D1542734

# INTERNATIONAL BUSINESS ETIQUETTE

## Latin America

*What You Need To Know To Conduct Business Abroad with Charm and Savvy*

By
Ann Marie Sabath

CAREER PRESS
Franklin Lakes, NJ

INTERNATIONAL BUSINESS ETIQUETTE:
LATIN AMERICA
Cover design by Design Solutions
Printed in the U.S.A. by Book-mart Press

To order this title, please call toll-free 1-800-CAREER-1 (NJ and Canada: 201-848-0310) to order using VISA or MasterCard, or for further information on books from Career Press.

The Career Press, Inc., 3 Tice Road, PO Box 687, Franklin Lakes, NJ 07417

**Library of Congress Cataloging-in-Publication Data**

Sabath, Ann Marie.
 International business etiquette. Latin America : what you need to
know to conduct business abroad with charm and savvy / by Ann Marie Sabath.
 p.   cm.
 Includes index.
 ISBN 1-56414-429-1 (paper)
 1. Business etiquette--Latin America. 2. National characteristics, Latin
American. 3. Intercultural communication. I. Title.

HF5389.3.L3 S22  2000
395.5'2'098--dc21

99-052267

# Acknowledgments

My acknowledgments go to...

My Syrian ancestors. They piqued my interest in Latin American culture and customs by immigrating to Argentina in the early 20th century.

That man of international vision, my publisher, Ron Fry.

My editor, Darren Bergstein, who transformed the manuscript into its finished form.

My literary agent, Brandon Toropov, who made this book a reality.

# Contents

# Introduction

Olé! Adelante! Arriba!

No matter where you are traveling in Latin America, you can be sure of one thing: the acceptable cultural mores often will vary greatly from those to which you may be accustomed. However, when you know what to expect and familiarize yourself with the proper manners and customs based on the country you will be visiting, you will feel more confident interacting with your international contacts.

This book is the third of my International Business Etiquette series. The first two books have addressed, respectively, the customs and manners of Europe, and Asia and the Pacific Rim. This book addresses the do's and don'ts when doing business in one or more of the 14 countries covered including Argentina, Bolivia, Brazil, Chile, Colombia, Costa Rica, Ecuador, Guatemala, Mexico, Panama, Paraguay, Peru, Uruguay, and Venezuela.

Like the first two books in this series, this one has been written to assist you in overcoming concerns you may have when confronted with a particular situation. It is meant to help you get that sand out of your international social gears so that it will be easier for you and your Latin American contacts to do business together.

Each chapter begins with a list of reasons why people do business in that particular country, as well as an overview and important facts and statistics regarding the country and its people. You will find some basic information regarding where you will land, what to wear based on climate, and the telephone codes that those you leave behind will want to have at their fingertips. You also will learn what to expect in your business dealings as you visit these countries—entertainment, dining, basic rules of conversation, when to tip and how much, customs and manners you should respect, and so on. In each chapter, you will learn such things as the real definition of punctuality for the country you're visiting, plus rules regarding seating arrangements, gift-giving, and the use of business cards. Special concerns for women are also addressed.

The following is a summary of the entire list of topics covered in each chapter.

# Statistics and Information

### Air Travel

When traveling abroad, the airport will be one of the first places you see. This section will tell you the name of the international airport where you are most likely to arrive. Many of the chapters also will suggest the most practical form of transportation for use from the airport to your destination.

### Country Codes

Among the many important facts regarding your trip that you will want to provide to both your family and your office staff are the telephone codes of where you will be. This section will give you codes for both the respective country and two or three major cities in each as well.

### Currency

If you have traveled abroad, you know that foreign currency often feels very much like monopoly money. This section offers the mean for you to familiarize yourself with the name of the bills and coins in each country. In addition, you will learn the denominations that are available for use, as well as the best places for currency exchange.

## Dates

You will find that there are two ways to write dates although in Latin America. One is by following the European Standard format, which consists of listing the number representing the day of the week followed by the number of the month and finally the two numbers representing the year. This section also will show you the appropriate way to write out dates, whether you are writing in longhand or are keying a letter on the computer. One thing to note: South Americans do not capitalize dates written out in longhand. For example, January would be written as *enero*.

## Ethnic Makeup

Many Latin American countries are made up of a variety of cultures. That includes both the descendants of immigrants who migrated to Latin America in the 19th and 20th centuries and individuals whose ancestors helped to build the country they are living in today. This section will help you to distinguish the mono or multicultural makeup of the Latin American country you are visiting. You will see that the populations of many countries are made up of *mestizos*, a people whose heritage is both European (usually Spanish) and Indian.

## Holidays and Religious Celebrations

Most Latin American countries have several holidays that are tied to either national commemorations or religious celebrations. These dates will be especially beneficial for you when planning a trip and determining the best time of year when you should or shouldn't travel.

## Language

Spanish is by far the predominant language in Latin American countries except for Brazil, where Portuguese holds that distinction. This section also will tell you in which countries you will hear English, French, German, and even some Indian dialects.

### Religion

This section details the religions practiced by the majority of Latin Americans. In some cases, it also will help you to see how religion is closely tied to Latin American lifestyles and beliefs.

### Time Zone Differences

Just as country codes are important, so are time zone differences. This section will help you to differentiate the time between the Latin American country you will be visiting and your home city. By knowing this information, you will be able to plan the best time to call home or inform others how to phone you at a convenient hour.

### Weather

Packing for your trip is contingent on the type of climate you should expect. This section will give you an idea of the type of clothes you'll need to pack based on the countries you will be visiting, particularly where you will be in those countries.

# Etiquette

### Business Attire

The way you look and what you wear are as important as who you are. Because many Latinos follow European fashion trends very closely, this section stresses the importance of dressing elegantly. It also emphasizes to travelers from the United States that although business casual dress may have a place in some situations, casual dress does not.

### Business Card Etiquette

Although there are no preset rules in Latin America regarding the exchange of business cards, this section stresses the importance of making sure you translate your cards into Spanish before leaving for your trip. You'll also learn what you should emphasize on your business card based on what is deemed important by your Latino contact.

## *Business Entertaining/Dining*

No matter where you travel in Latin America, you will find that your business relationships will be based on how well you have interacted with your contacts in social settings.

Much of this time spent together will be during meals. This section will tell you which meals are considered the main courses of the day (based on the country you are visiting) and when you should expect to eat them. Tips regarding table manners will be offered. Finally, you will learn what your Latin American contacts will expect of you when you are either hosting a meal or are their guest.

## *Conversation*

One of the best attributes of Latin Americans is their friendly manner. As you are establishing rapport with your in-country contacts, "small talk" will be important. This section will share with you the best topics of conversation to pursue and those to avoid.

## *Gestures and Public Manners*

Many mannerisms that are considered acceptable in your homeland may be thought of as offensive in Latin America. Conversely, you might ordinarily never consider engaging in the manners and gestures that you will be encouraged to use from this book. This section will assist you in learning what is and is not appropriate public behavior, including all forms of nonverbal communication.

## *Gift-Giving Etiquette*

Although gift-giving is not the ritual in Latin America that it is in other parts of the world, it still is an important part of the rapport-developing process. This section will tell you the best types of gifts to give your Latin American contacts and when those presents should be given. You also will learn what *not* to give so that you don't unknowingly offend the person with whom you are trying to develop a working relationship.

### Greetings and Introductions

First impressions make a big difference around the globe. One of the first forms of establishing rapport will be when you meet and greet your Latin American contacts. This section will share such tips as when you should prepare to shake hands and the proper distance to stand from a person. You will also learn when to expect an embrace and perhaps even a kiss, and who should initiate such gestures.

### Hierarchy Is Important

Although most corporations have organizational charts, some of them may not be seen by individuals from outside the company. For that reason, this section has been created to assist you in determining who is the highest person on the totem pole or who has the most decision-making power.

### How Decisions Are Made

In many Latin American countries, you will find that the person making the final decision may not even be at initial meetings. You also will find that having the best product, service, or price may not be the determining factor for who ends up winning that sought-after business. This section will help you to understand how Latin Americans draw conclusions about who should earn their business and what you should do so that you are the person who earns it.

### Meeting Manners

A meeting is a meeting is a meeting, or so you would think—until you've attended a meeting in Latin America. This section will teach you that meetings come in many forms. For instance, you will find that it is common to have meetings without a pre-established agenda in some countries, whereas in others the agenda on the table may not even be followed.

### Punctuality

There is a Spanish saying, "El tiempo es como es espacio" or "time is space." Many Latin Americans see time as fluid, allowing the situation at hand to take precedence over scheduled appointments. This section guides you in matters of punctuality, which most likely will be a loose arrangement in the country you are visiting.

### Seating Etiquette

In most of the Latin American countries in this book, there is a common way to sit at a table, whether it is in a conference room or in a restaurant. This section will describe where you should expect to be offered a seat when you are a guest, as well as where to seat others (including yourself) when you are the host.

### Tipping Tips

As in countries around the world, whom to tip and how much to give varies throughout Latin America. This section will help you to overcome those moments of hesitation when you don't know what is appropriate or even when tipping may not be necessary. Rather than allowing you to commit a faux pas, this section has been included to give you a few essential guidelines.

### Toasting Etiquette

"Salud!" is a term that will get you far in Latin America. Although you will be drinking wine in many Latin American countries, in others, toasts may be proposed with a beer or other alcoholic beverage in hand. This section will assist you in feeling more comfortable during these situations.

### When You Are Invited to a Home

Although most business entertaining will be conducted in restaurants, you may have the honor of being invited to the home of your Latin American contact. When this is the case, you will want to know when to arrive, what to expect once you get there, and what to bring with you.

### Women in Business

Many Latin American women have made great strides in the business world; others have not yet achieved major opportunities. This section will assist women traveling to Latin America in learning how to earn the respect of their Latin American associates, as well as how they should expect to be treated in any particular country.

### Whatever You Do...

This section is at the end of each chapter. It is meant to be a quick review of the "don'ts" of each country covered. Some "don'ts" are common throughout the continent, although others are unique to a particular nation. In either case, this section will help you to stay on the good side of your Latin American hosts.

# Chapter 1

# Argentina

---

### 7 reasons people do business in Argentina

1. Argentina is one of the wealthiest nations in South America.

2. Argentine businesspeople spend more hours in the office than their U.S., European, and Japanese counterparts.

3. Argentina's top imports include computers.

4. Argentina is one of the world's largest producers of wine, for which it is internationally renowned.

5. Food processing and agribusiness are Argentina's two largest industries.

6. Argentina has one of the lowest inflation rates in the world.

7. Argentina's citizens are multiethnic, providing greater diversity and therefore greater business opportunities.

---

The Argentine Republic—known in the United States simply as Argentina—is the eighth largest country in the world, and in South America is second in size only to Brazil. Together, Argentina and Chile form the long tail of the South American continent, with Chile skirting the Pacific Ocean on the western side and Argentina bordering the Atlantic Ocean on the east; the Andean Cordilleras mountain range separates the two countries. Argentina also is bordered by Uruguay, Brazil, and Paraguay to the northeast and Bolivia to the north. Control over the island territory of Tierra del Fuego (located at the very tip of the continent) is shared with Chile.

Geographically, the country generally is divided into four primary areas: the Andes in the west, an area that includes the Lake District; the northern section that is called Mesopotamia, rich with tropical rainforests; the alternately dry and humid Pampas in the central portion of the country; and Patagonia in the south and southeast, throughout which you will find both steppes and glaciers. The capital of Buenos Aires lies on the east coast, in the mouth of the Rio de la Plata. Argentina is very popular with tourists, who are drawn to such highlights as the tango, its best-known and most popular dance, and who visit the country's many natural wonders, including the famous Iguazu Falls and the Moreno Glacier.

Of all the countries in Latin America, you will find Argentina to be the most European, with the vast majority of its population of

34 million composed of Italian, Yugoslavian, French, German, and British immigrants, as well as Eastern European Jews. This has inevitably created a continental influence that makes Argentina very appealing to foreigners wishing to do business there. Of all the Latin American countries, in fact, this is probably the place where U.S. and European businesspeople will feel most "at home."

On the other hand, Argentina's history of political turmoil has had its effect on the economic landscape. This includes a revolution in the early 1800s that led to the country's independence from Spain, and a military coup in 1943 that brought about Juan Perón's rise to power and subsequent dictatorship. (Perón's wife, Eva, became a popular icon, not just in Argentina but throughout the world, and played a large role in his success.) Perón was himself deposed and exiled in 1955, then returned to power in 1973 before passing away in 1974. His third wife, Isabel, succeeded him, but her government crumbled in 1976. From 1976 to 1983, a vicious military government ran roughshod over the Argentine population, and close to 30,000 citizens disappeared during this period, which has been called the "Dirty War."

With the country falling apart both politically and economically, the situation began to change when Argentina entered into a war with Great Britain over ownership of the Malvinas (aka Falkland) Islands, located in the Atlantic Ocean several hundred miles off the Argentine Coast. Although the Malvinas still remain in dispute, the war had the happy effect of bringing about the downfall of the ignominious military government and a return to the constitution of 1853.

Argentina is now a republic headed by an elected president, Carlos Saúl Menem, and governed by the bicameral National Congress. The Peronistas have the strongest political influence in the country. Economically, Argentina has made a dramatic recovery because the dark days of the late 1970s and early 1980s, although it still has some obstacles to overcome, including an unemployment rate of nearly 14 percent. Overall, however, the country has become quite stable and is a real attraction for foreign investors.

# Statistics and Information

### Air Travel

When arriving in Buenos Aires (or "good airs") by plane, you will land at the Ezelza International Airport, or EZE, less than 25 miles from Buenos Aires. If you don't have a lot of luggage, an airport bus is a cost-effective method of transportation from the airport into the city. Otherwise, taking a taxi is the most practical way to get to your hotel.

### Country Codes

Argentina's country code is 54.

Key city codes:

- 11 for Buenos Aires.
- 351 for Cordoba.
- 341 for Rosario.
- 261 for Mendoza.

### Currency

Argentina's unit of currency is called the *peso*; these bills circulate in denominations of 1,000, 100, 50, 10, 5, and 1. The Argentine coin is called the *centavo*; 100 *centavos* equals 1 *peso*. The *centavo* is found in denominations of 50, 10, 5, and 1/2.

United States currency is widely accepted throughout Argentina, more so than any other foreign currency. Besides being able to exchange your dollars in hotels or with travel agents, credit cards such as Visa, MasterCard, and American Express also are accepted in many parts of Argentina.

Although traveler's checks can be exchanged in urban centers, you may have difficulty cashing them in less-populated areas.

## Dates

There are two ways of writing dates in Argentina. When writing in longhand, it is appropriate to start with the day of the week, then the number of the date, followed by the month, and finally the year. For example, Friday, July 23, 2001 should be written as *viernes*, 23 de *julio* de 2001.

Similarly, if you are listing the date in numeric form, the appropriate way would be to write first the day of the month followed by the number of the month and then the year. Thus, July 23, 2001 would be written as 23/07/01.

## Ethnic Makeup

Argentina contains few indigenous people; approximately 85 percent of the population are European descendants (primarily Spain, Italy, Germany, and England), although the remaining 15 percent are comprised of mestizo (see Introduction), Indian, and some other minorities.

## Holidays and Religious Celebrations

| | |
|---|---|
| January 1 | New Year's Day |
| May 1 | Labor Day |
| May 25 | Independence Day (also called Revolution Day) |
| June 10 | Sovereignty Day (also called Malvinas Day) |
| June 20 | National Independence Day |
| July 9 | Memorial to General Jose de San Martín, Argentina's liberator |
| October 12 | Columbus Day |
| December 25 | Christmas Day |

*Note:* If you are planning to visit Argentina, keep in mind that January, February, and the second and third week of July typically are reserved for vacations. Plus, a number of businesses close during these periods and most employees vacate their office for approximately two weeks.

## Language

The official language of Argentina is the *castellano* or *castillian* form of Spanish. *Lunfardo* is a slang language that is also rather common; it originated as a result of people using a combination of Spanish, Italian, French, and English terms.

English is used by individuals in the corporate sector, making it Argentina's business language. You also will hear German, French, Italian, and some Indian dialects spoken throughout the country.

## Religion

More than 90 percent of Argentina's population practice Roman Catholicism. Less than 3 percent are Protestant, with about 2 percent following Judaism. Other religions, including Ukranian Catholic and Armenian Orthodox, are also practiced though in smaller numbers.

## Time Zone Differences

Argentina is:

- Three hours behind Greenwich Mean Time.
- Two hours ahead of U.S. Eastern Standard Time.

## Weather

In the more heavily populated central region of the country, Argentina has a temperate climate, with cold winters and hot summers. However, Argentina's weather is as diverse as the country is vast. From the near-Antarctic south to the subtropical north, from the tops of the Andes to the beaches that envelope the country, a variety of climates are available for those who seek them.

If you are doing business in Buenos Aires, be warned that the weather there can be extremely hot and humid from about mid-December to the end of February, with temperatures ranging as high as 95°. The best time of year to be in Buenos Aires is during the winter months of June, July, and August.

# Etiquette

### Business Attire

With its sense of fashion and cosmopolitan air, Buenos Aires has become known as the Paris of Latin America. One reason for this is that Argentines place a high value on the style and quality of their clothes—something to be kept in mind as you pack for your trip.

In business situations, it is considered appropriate for men to wear conservative dark suits and ties. Women should also wear conservative yet elegant business suits, skirts and blouses, or dresses.

### Business Card Etiquette

It is common to exchange business cards in Argentina; however, no specific rules or regulations apply. Simply take note of the business card you have received and express your thanks.

Although the majority of businesspeople in Argentina are quite fluent in English, having your card translated in Spanish on the opposite side will be greatly appreciated.

### Business Entertaining/Dining

Argentines believe that building and developing trust with individuals is paramount for establishing business relationships. One way that these relationships are developed is by spending time together during meals. Business dinners are the norm, because many Argentines return to their homes for lunch.

When you are invited to dinner, prepare to meet around 10 p.m. and to be together for at least two hours. Conversation will focus most likely on social topics rather than the business at hand. Wait to discuss business only if it is brought up by your host; otherwise, you may risk offending your Argentine contact.

Beef is a very common meat in Argentina. However, you should expect to be served some foods that may be slightly different than the cuisine to which you are accustomed—for example, cow brains, intestines, kidneys, and so on. Even if you've never wanted to try these foods before, it is considered proper to at least taste them rather than to risk offending your Argentine host by refusing them. Besides, you can always make up for it with special culinary treats, including the delicious *helado*, which is Argentinian ice cream.

*Table manners:* As in other Latin American countries, the continental style of using utensils is adopted in Argentina—that is, keep your fork in your left hand with the tines down and your knife in your right hand with the serrated edge facing the plate. When not using your utensils, be sure to keep your hands on the table at all times, as hands below the table is considered poor manners. To signal that you have finished eating, lay your knife and fork parallel on the plate, with the handles to the right.

If you are invited to join your Argentine contact between 4 p.m. and 6 p.m., then you will probably be enjoying "tea." This will most likely be comprised of coffee (which may taste like espresso to North Americans) and dessert foods.

Because Argentines are a very proud people, they may insist on paying the bill whether or not they have initiated the meal invitation. When you are hosting the meal, in order to prevent a "tug of war," you should make arrangements with the wait staff to pay for the meal beforehand or by excusing yourself from the table at an appropriate moment. If you are not able to do this, then you may have to insist repeatedly on paying the bill.

If you are a woman, note that *machismo* is very prevalent in Argentina. Therefore, an Argentine man would be very embarrassed if a women paid for the meal or even offered to pay for the meal. As a female host, if you wish to pay the bill, it is best to arrange for a male associate or family member to take care of it on your behalf.

Finally, as in many countries, do not wait for the server to bring the bill to the table; it will be presented only after you request it.

## Conversation

It won't take long to find out that Argentines enjoy making small talk; as a rule, they are very sociable and culturally oriented people. Appropriate topics of conversation include the arts, sports such as *futbol* (soccer), the area of Argentina you are visiting, wine, your international travels, and restaurants.

Women may find themselves asked personal questions that could seem indiscreet or even rude—for example: "How much do you weigh?" or "Are you married?" It is important to keep in mind that this is part of the Argentine culture. If you are a woman and are asked these types of questions, try to avoid expressing frustration or anger, and answer them as discreetly as possible.

You should avoid asking questions about family and personal life until you have become better acquainted with the other person. In addition, although many Argentines enjoy discussing politics and religion, you should initially avoid these topics, because this nationality tends to have very strong opinions and conversation can become heated. You also should avoid asking an Argentine if he or she has Indian roots, as this question will be misinterpreted as an insult.

Finally, avoid making any derogatory remarks about Argentina's government, its cities, or its sports teams. As in any situation, you are better off when you accentuate the positive over the negative.

## Gestures and Public Manners

The Argentine people are expressive and affectionate. They also have different concepts of personal space than that to which people from other cultures may be accustomed, and they can be touchy about negative reactions to their expressiveness. Therefore, when interacting with the Argentines, be careful not to take offense at such actions as arm touching and shoulder pats, and be sure not to back away if you feel as though your space is being invaded. If you do, your Argentine contact may label you as cold or impersonal.

Some rules of thumb are necessary for interacting with Argentines. For instance, do not put your hands on your hips when talking to others; you could be perceived as being overly assertive. Another gesture to avoid is hitting your right fist and left palm together although speaking with someone. This communicates disbelief or insinuates "That's stupid." In addition, do not make the "okay" sign (thumb and index finger connected) or the "thumbs up" sign; these are profane gestures in Argentina.

Good eye contact is a must for registering interest. Women should be careful, however, that their eye contact with men is not misinterpreted as displaying a romantic interest.

Be aware that it is considered rude to eat in any public place other than a restaurant. Do not indulge in any "snacking" although walking the streets or riding public transportation. When in a cafe, if you would like a beverage in a cup, let your server know by cupping your hands together.

Smoking is prevalent in Argentina, as it is throughout other Latin American countries. If you are a smoker, be sure to follow proper smoking protocol by first offering a cigarette to those around you before lighting up yourself.

## Gift-Giving Etiquette

Unlike many countries in other parts of the world, gifts are generally not exchanged with your Argentine counterpart at the beginning of a business relationship. Once you've established such a relationship, however, it is appropriate to send your associate a quality gift such as a pen or desk clock.

It is an honor to be invited to the home of an Argentine, and you should certainly go with something in hand. Suitable gifts for the hostess include flowers, chocolates, pastries, scotch (referred to as whiskey in Argentina), and other imported liquors.

## Greetings and Introductions

Shaking hands is important when meeting and greeting others in most nations, and this is certainly the case with Argentines. For that reason, be sure to extend your hand to everyone you meet, both when you're saying hello and upon departure. Bear in mind that first impressions are important to Argentines; be sure to make your handshake both confident and inviting. Protocol dictates that women should initiate all handshakes with men.

After you have met your Argentine contact a few times, prepare to be greeted with a kiss thereafter. This is a way of expressing the rapport that has been established between you. In business and social situations, it is common for women to greet each other with both a kiss on each cheek and also by shaking hands upon introduction.

Argentines will appreciate it if you use their titles when addressing them—for example, "Doctor," "Engineer," "Professor," and so on. Using titles demonstrates your respect.

Although sustained eye contact can be intimidating to some, this is not the case with Argentines. In their culture, eye contact is a very important part of letting others know you are interested in what they have to say. Thus, maintaining eye contact will be an important part of establishing rapport.

The power of a smile is just as important as eye contact. In fact, this form of nonverbal communication will go a long way with your Argentine contacts.

At large gatherings, it is considered appropriate to introduce yourself if others aren't around to make introductions. However, at smaller get-togethers, wait for the person hosting the function to introduce you to other guests.

When greeting others, extend your respect to the most senior person present by acknowledging him or her first.

## *Hierarchy Is Important*

Although developing relationships with individuals at all levels is important in Argentina, it is especially important to recognize and respect hierarchy and to remember that top executives play an important role in final decisions (see *How Decisions are Made*).

On the other side of the coin, your professional status and ranking will be important to your Argentine contacts. You will find, in fact, that senior executives and people of status always are given the most respect in any setting. Argentines are especially impressed with others' accomplishments. Thus, your professional achievements and financial status will all play a vital role in Argentine society.

Grandparents and other senior citizens are held in high esteem in Argentina. In fact, children are raised with the understanding that a great deal of respect should be shown to their *abuelos* (grandparents) and other elders. You should do your best to demonstrate equal respect.

## *How Decisions Are Made*

When it comes to making decisions, the hierarchical structure in Argentine business is similar to that in the United States. You will find that senior management has the "last word," and that any decision is often based on the personal preferences of the key decision-maker rather than on the quality of the product or service being purchased. For this reason, it follows that if your personal relationship is solid with your Argentine contact in senior management, you will have a better chance to develop a working relationship with the organization that person represents.

When a decision is close to being made, remember that *what* you know is important, but *who* you know is much more so.

## Meeting Manners

Although Argentines are a very social and even playful people, they also have a serious and somber side. In business, it is important that you recognize this. When you first engage in a meeting, you should allow time for your associates to "warm up" to you. A solid relationship must be built before business can be transacted. For that reason, kibbutzing typically precedes getting down to business.

Smiling and making small talk are vital to establishing a business rapport. However, don't ever assume you can joke with an Argentine from the start; if you do, your meeting may end before it begins. To imply that someone or something is not to be taken seriously is a great insult in Argentina.

When you enter the meeting room, wait for someone to seat you. Individuals with the highest rank are typically seated across from one another.

Be prepared for discussions and for decisions to take time. In fact, it is very likely that you will have to engage in several meetings before a decision is made.

*Note:* Because the process moves so slowly, be sure not to oversell your product or idea; instead, you will find it more effective to move in a slow and steadfast manner.

## Punctuality

When you are invited to a home, prepare to arrive around 30 to 45 minutes later than the time given on the invitation; it would be inappropriate to arrive early or even on time.

Although time is fluid to most Argentines, you will be expected to be on time for business meetings. Don't be surprised, however, if you are kept waiting 30 to 45 minutes. If this happens, do not display impatience or show any indication that you feel your time is being wasted. To bridge the time gap, bring along some reading material or something productive to do.

Always, however, arrive on time for meetings held at restaurants. In this case, you can expect your Argentinian associate to be prompt.

### Seating Etiquette

Seating etiquette in Argentina dictates that the host and hostess sit at either end of the table. In turn, the most senior woman will be seated to the right of the host, with the most senior man seated to the right of the hostess. In a business situation, those with the highest rank typically are seated across from one another.

### Tipping Tips

You may expect restaurant bills to include a gratuity. For that reason, tipping is unnecessary. However, if you have been extremely pleased with the service or have made special requests, leaving an additional 5 percent tip would be appropriate.

When you are in a hotel and a bellman helps you with your luggage, it is in order to tip the equivalent of $1 for each bag that is handled.

When you take a taxi, it is not required that you tip the driver. If you decide to tip, however, around 50 centavos is appropriate.

A tip of 25 to 50 centavos is appropriate for an airport porter who has given you assistance.

When you attend the theater, prepare to tip the usher 5 percent of the ticket price.

### Toasting Etiquette

Wait until a toast is made before you begin drinking, or until others have begun to drink. Argentines typically toast with the term "Salud!"

### When You Are Invited to a Home

It is extremely rare to be invited to a home, because most Argentines prefer to entertain in restaurants. For that reason, consider it an honor if you are invited to someone's home. Also prepare to enjoy a late dinner, because this meal is commonly taken around 10 p.m.

You should always bring a gift for the hostess; flowers and chocolates are quite appropriate.

Never leave immediately following the completion of dinner and dessert; you should stay a minimum of one-and-a-half hours afterwards to socialize.

If there are children in the home, make a point of admiring and complimenting them.

### Whatever You Do...

- Don't refer to an Argentine as an Indian or ask if he or she is of Indian descent.
- Don't criticize or joke about the Argentine culture or traditions.
- Don't expect an Argentine to put business before family or relationships.
- Don't eat food as you are walking in public.
- Don't necessarily trust the directions you receive from an Argentine as exact. Frequently, Argentines will give you directions even if they don't really know them, rather then losing face by admitting their ignorance.

- Don't wear shorts when you are walking around in public (unless you don't want to be taken seriously). Argentines take great pride in their physical appearance, which reflects their taste in fashion. You will find that Argentines almost always dress in a fairly conservative manner, even when simply shopping or taking an afternoon walk.

- Don't become offended if someone jokes with you, even if it concerns your appearance or weight.

- If you are a woman, don't go out alone at night or into bars.

- Don't forget to show interest in and respect for the Argentine culture.

# Chapter 2

# Bolivia

## 8 reasons people do business in Bolivia

1.  As a country that is yet to be discovered by large corporations,
    Bolivia awaits creative and ambitious entrepreneurs.

2.  Bolivia has managed to maintain a very low crime rate throughout the years; it has a reputation for being one of the safest countries in the world.

3.  The country has a rich culture and beautifully diverse terrain.

4.  Bolivia lies in the center of South America, making it the ideal location for land-based business with other Latin American countries.

5.  Bolivia's people are open to innovative ideas, especially those that can be incorporated into the present culture.

6.  Bolivia is home to the world's highest ski run and golf course.

7.  Friendship is a priority in Bolivia, and its people are concerned with the welfare of others.

8.  Bolivia has several prime industries, including agriculture, tin mining, and natural gas, and is a major trading partner with the United States.

In many ways the centerpiece of South America, the land-locked Republic of Bolivia is simultaneously one of the poorest and richest countries on the continent. Due to its altitude and isolation, Bolivia has often been described as "the Tibet of the Americas."

But this has as much to do with its culture as with its geographical location. Bolivia holds a great deal of fascination for travelers, chiefly due to a history dating back thousands of years that can be detected in the ruins of ancient civilizations found throughout the country, and in the indigenous Indian population that continues to hold tight to traditions and beliefs that are often at odds with modern society.

Unlike many other Latin American countries, only about 10 percent of Bolivia's population of 7.8 million people consist of European immigrants; the rest are composed of Indian tribes and mestizo. That it has retained so much of its ethnic heritage is due in large part to its location, tucked inside a grouping of numerous other South American countries. To the west, Peru and Chili separate it from the Pacific Ocean, Although Brazil lies on its north and east borders, Paraguay on the southeast, and Argentina on the south.

The fifth largest country on the continent, Bolivia has a history of outside invasion and having its borders constantly rearranged. Originally part of the Incan empire, the land was conquered by Spain in the 1500s and remained under Spanish rule until 1825 when, after years of resistance and revolution led by Simón Bolívar and his lieutenant, Antonio José de Sucre, a republic was declared. However, the country continued to fight battles with neighbors that coveted its rich land and natural resources. As a result, Bolivia lost much of its original boundaries, primarily to Chile and Paraguay.

Bolivia also has suffered many domestic troubles, including a succession of civilian and military regimes throughout the 20th century, creating an instability that has been overcome in recent years by electing a president and establishing a democratic government.

Economically, the poverty-stricken country has been hurt by years of hyperinflation, which is now being brought under control but has in the past made Bolivia unattractive to foreign investors. Further complicating matters is the fact that Bolivia is the world's second-largest exporter of cocaine, thus jeopardizing its relationship with the United States.

On the plus side, Bolivia has a strong agricultural industry (the second largest in South America) that provides employment for a good portion of its population and has many industrial opportunities yet to be explored and exploited by foreign investors.

# Statistics and Information

### Country Codes

Bolivia's country code is 591.

City codes:

- 2 for La Paz.
- 3 for Santa Cruz.

## Currency

The unit of currency in Bolivia is the *boliviano,* which comes in bills of 200, 100, 50, 10, 5, and 2. Coins circulate in 1 *boliviano* and 50, 20, 10, 5, and 2 *centavos.* One *boliviano* equals 100 *centavos.*

U.S. dollars are the only foreign currency accepted throughout the country, although others may be exchanged at the borders. Money can be changed in travel agencies, jewelry stores, and pharmacies. Major credit cards may be used in larger cities.

## Dates

Like other Latin Americans, Bolivians write their dates in the European format of day, month, and year. For example, January 30, 1999 is written as 30/1/99.

## Ethnic Makeup

Bolivia's population tops out at about 8 million, with the majority composed of indigenous people including Quechua Indian (approximately 30 percent), mestizo (28 percent), and Aymará Indian (25 percent). Approximately 10 percent of Bolivians are of European (primarily Spanish) descent.

## Holidays and Religious Celebrations

| | |
|---|---|
| January 1 | New Year's Day |
| February/March | Carnival |
| March/April | Good Friday and Easter Sunday |
| May 1 | Labor Day |
| May 25 | Independence Day (separated from Spain) |
| June (varies) | Corpus Christi |
| August 6 | Independence Day (official independence from Spain) |
| November 1 | All Saints' Day |
| December 25 | Christmas Day |

*Note:* Carnival is celebrated widely with music, food, dancing, and festivities. Part of the Carnival tradition is that anyone within throwing distance is subject to be hit by a water balloon.

## Language

The official language of Bolivia is Spanish, although no more than 70 percent of the population speak it. *Quechua* (the second most common language) and Aymará are Indian languages also spoken by Bolivians, in addition to composite dialects. Indigenous people typically speak their own languages.

## Religion

The majority of people (about 95 percent) practice Roman Catholicism, but most of those follow a hybrid form that integrates many Inca and Aymará rites and beliefs. The other 5 percent of the population is a mixture of many different religions, including those of the indigenous Indian tribes.

## Time Zone Differences

Bolivia is:
- Four hours behind Greenwich Mean Time.
- One hour ahead U.S. Eastern Standard Time.

## Weather

Due to the various altitudes in Bolivia, one can find a wide range of temperatures, from tropical to very cold, and from humid to somewhat dry. For example, because of its altitude, the city of La Paz is cold throughout the year, whereas Santa Cruz varies from warm to hot, and the city of Cochabamba maintains a moderate temperature.

Your best bet is to research the city you will be visiting in order to determine the appropriate dress for that climate.

# Etiquette

### Business Attire

As previously mentioned, it will benefit you to research the climate of your destination to best determine what you will need for your trip. Business dress varies throughout Bolivia, depending on the city and temperature.

In the city of La Paz, men typically take the conservative approach; a three-piece suit (black, navy blue, or charcoal gray) is the norm. Men in Cochabamba also wear conservative, dark-colored suits, but two-piece suits are more common. Because of the consistently warm temperature in Santa Cruz, men in that city lean toward lightweight suits.

Appropriate dress for businesswomen includes skirts and blouses, business suits, and dresses. Women who wear conservative, unrevealing attire are seen as more professional and are treated accordingly.

Avoid clothing and accessories that may be interpreted as Indian, as Native Indians often feel that foreigners are mocking them by wearing such attire. Note that this includes bowler hats, which are commonly worn by Indian women.

It is important to remember that because the temperature may vary, so may acceptable dress rules. Play it safe and mirror the dress of your Bolivian counterparts.

### Business Card Etiquette

Always have business cards with you when interacting with your Bolivian counterparts. Even though many Bolivian professionals will speak English (especially the upper level executives), you should have the Spanish equivalent of your card printed on the opposite side.

Avoid seeming arrogant or boastful when handing out your business cards. Similarly, be attentive, appreciative, and respectful when receiving someone else's business card.

## Business Entertaining/Dining

It is common for Bolivians to discuss business Although dining. As a rule of thumb, however, you should wait for your host to initiate the business conversation.

If the sole intent of your interaction is to discuss business, it is more likely that you will meet over lunch. If your mutual intent involves entertainment and building a business relationship, then dinner is more the norm.

More times than not, when entertaining or being entertained, only those directly involved in negotiations or the development of a business relationship are involved in lunch or dinner meetings.

If you are the host, keep in mind that Bolivians prefer restaurants where native food is served. The most popular cuisine in Bolivia centers around meat dishes, most often accompanied by potatoes or rice, plus shredded lettuce. Watch out for a hot sauce called *llajhua*, which is often added to favorite dishes.

Although in some countries it is considered polite to leave something on your plate (and for the uninformed, the United States happens to be one of those countries), Bolivia can be considered to be a member of the "clean plate club." Leaving food on your plate is considered wasteful.

The host is typically expected to pay for the meal. A 10 percent gratuity will usually be added into the bill; it is common, however, to leave another 5 percent to let your waiter know you were pleased with the service.

Be sure to brush up on your table manners. Your Bolivian counterparts may not be particularly judgmental, but it can only help to know your do's and don'ts when dining.

Be prepared when invited out to drink. Bolivians are nothing if not hearty in their drinking habits, and you may find Bolivian beer and wine overwhelming, to say the least. A native specialty, in fact, is a hard liquor made from maize called *chicha*.

Friday evenings are referred to as *viernes de soltero*, or bachelor Friday. Bolivian women believe men will be nicer throughout the week if they go out with their male friends every Friday evening to drink and party. As a rule, women do not accompany men on these occasions.

### *Conversation*

The emphasis Bolivians place on friendship will be evident by their love of conversation. Good topics of conversation include Bolivian culture, food, families, and sports such as auto racing and soccer. Be sure to ask about the city you're visiting, including its local traditions and festivities.

Try to brush up on your knowledge of Bolivia's national sports teams and culture. By doing this, you are sure to score some "brownie points" with your Bolivian colleagues.

Be ready and willing to answer questions about yourself, your family, and the country and region you live in. Whether answering questions or engaging in a discussion, be sure to always focus on the positive instead of the negative.

*Topics to avoid:* Politics (on any level), religion, drugs or drug policies, social classes, any U.S. military involvement in Bolivia, and any comparisons between Bolivia and the United States. These topics are considered by many to be sensitive areas in which Bolivians tend to have very strong opinions.

You should be aware that Bolivia has often engaged in wars with its surrounding neighbors. As a result, one should avoid discussions concerning Chile, Peru, Brazil, and Argentina.

Never ask a Bolivian if he or she is of Indian descent. Even though many Bolivians contain some percentage of Indian in their ancestry, they often choose to identify with their Spanish heritage instead.

## Gestures and Public Manners

Be aware that Bolivians will greatly appreciate any effort you make to use Spanish, so if you are unfamiliar with the language, make the effort to learn a few terms.

Be sure to maintain eye contact with Bolivians both when they are talking to you and when you are speaking to them. If you don't, they may misinterpret this as disinterest.

Do not eat as you walk; this is considered a sign of bad manners in Bolivia. If you purchase something to snack on when you are outdoors, look for a place to stop and eat it before continuing.

You may think it is harmless to speak in a low voice to the person next to you, but in Bolivia this is very rude, because those around you may believe that you are talking about them. For that reason, avoid "private" discussions and choose your topics of conversation carefully so that everyone in the group can participate.

Be sure to display deference to higher-ranking individuals in any corporation. One way to do this is to make a point of directing your questions and responses to these people. You can also use nonverbal forms of communication such as eye contact, tone of voice, and a respectful attitude.

*Note*: Recognizing an individual's higher rank should not be achieved at the expense of other, lower-ranking counterparts. Remember to treat *everyone* with respect; Bolivians value the opinions of their co-workers and so should you.

## Gift-Giving Etiquette

When invited to a home, be sure to bring a gift. Expensive alcoholic beverages such as wine or whiskey are appreciated. Good candy, chocolates, and flowers are also favorable gifts. Note: Do *not* give purple and yellow flowers, as these are considered morbid colors in Bolivia.

If you know that your host has children, be sure to acknowledge them by presenting candy, games, or small toys. *Note*: When it comes to children, candy is your safest bet, especially sweets that are less attainable, such as North American candy.

In a business situation, your Bolivian counterpart will appreciate receiving quality notebooks, calendars, organizers, literature, and nice pens. *Important*: Avoid giving gifts that contain your company logo, as this may be perceived as arrogant.

Do not expect the other person to open the gift in your presence. Bolivians appreciate the act of gift-giving more than the gift itself.

### *Greetings and Introductions*

Always offer a warm handshake to others when arriving and departing.

In a group situation, be sure to acknowledge and make small talk with each person individually. In Bolivia, it is considered rude and impersonal to acknowledge people as a group ("Hello everybody!") as opposed to one-on-one interactions.

In initial greetings, it is common for good friends to embrace and kiss one another on both sides of the cheek.

As noted in "Gestures and Public Manners," it is important to practice good eye contact when meeting and speaking with people.

Make a point of using people's academic and professional titles; this is very important to Bolivians. A person's title should be followed by his or her last name. For example, a college graduate or lawyer has the title of *Licenciado*. Thus, Juan Valdez would be referred to as *Licenciado* Valdez.

Note that it is recommended you learn the correct pronunciation of Bolivian names and titles. It may be considered a grave insult if you mispronounce either one.

Pay special attention to people of importance or higher professional ranking.

### Hierarchy Is Important

Hierarchy is more important than it may first appear in Bolivia. Power and status is desired and respected from both a business and social standpoint.

Upper level executives make the decisions (big and small) within Bolivian companies. Thus, if you want to accomplish anything in Bolivia's corporate culture, you need to go to the top.

As is true in many other countries, money, education, and your professional standing will all play a role in making you a prominent figure in Bolivian society.

### How Decisions Are Made

Compared to the United States, the decision-making process in Bolivia is quite lengthy. Business negotiations often require several meetings and business trips, as Bolivians will typically end negotiations before allowing themselves to be hurried into a business commitment.

Your best tactic during this drawn-out process is to remain calm and tolerant.

Here are two important pointers that will assist you throughout the negotiation process:

- Be patient. Corporate culture in Bolivia can be very bureaucratic. Often your most important contacts and business relationships are those for which you wait the longest.
- Recognize the power of personal referrals. A phone call, letter, or face-to-face visit from a third party can often cut through the "red tape" you will encounter.

### Meeting Manners

It is important to remember that Latin Americans have a relaxed concept of time compared to North Americans. It is best to "pace" yourself; scheduling different meetings back-to-back will only create chaos.

Be prepared to sit through several face-to-face meetings throughout any business negotiation process in Bolivia.

Be sure to engage in small talk before and after the meeting. This will communicate that you value your personal relationships even more than the business you are there to discuss.

Have all your written materials and handouts translated into Spanish. It may also be helpful to have an interpreter with you, as many educated Bolivians do not speak English.

You may ensure responsiveness from your Bolivian counterparts through the use of visual and well-composed presentations. Do whatever you can to make your presentation look colorful, interesting, and attractive.

During the meeting, be sure to maintain good eye contact with your audience, and especially with the top executives. Nonverbal communication with key decision makers will boost your apparent awareness of their power and status.

As is true in most countries, your presentation of a gracious attitude, nice wardrobe, and proper etiquette will aid your ability to form business relationships.

## *Punctuality*

To the Bolivians, punctuality is unimportant and takes a "back seat" to personal needs and relationships. Some Bolivians may be sensitive to the corporate culture of North Americans and will therefore arrive promptly for business meetings.

However, you should play it safe and not expect your Bolivian counterpart to be punctual, as it is very unlikely that a business meeting will start on time. Similarly, very little importance is placed on deadlines.

Note that the more important the person is, the less punctual they may in fact be. If you are scheduled to meet with a top-level executive, you may be left sitting outside that person's office for hours. It could happen that the executive may finally be able to see you only to ask if the meeting can be rescheduled.

As the visitor, you should always arrive for meetings promptly, no matter whether others are late. Always be punctual when meeting in a restaurant.

Never arrive early for a social occasion, as this is considered to be very rude. Instead, plan on arriving at least 30 minutes late.

### Seating Etiquette

In any table setting, the head of the table is reserved for the host and hostess. The highest-ranking man in your organization will be asked to sit to the immediate right of the hostess, Although the highest-ranking woman will be seated to the immediate right of the host.

### Tipping Tips

Because the majority of taxi drivers own their vehicle, it is only necessary to tip them for long trips. In such a case, a few dollars should be sufficient. *Important:* Be sure to inquire into the cost of a trip before you set out on any taxi ride.

A 10 percent gratuity is typically included in restaurant bills. If you were pleased with the service, tipping an extra 5 percent is both appropriate and appreciated.

Tip airport porters $1 for each bag they handle.

### Toasting Etiquette

Just as in other Latin American countries, the appropriate term to use for toasting is "Salud!" When you are toasted, be sure to propose one in return.

## *When You Are Invited to a Home*

Consider it an honor if you are invited to a Bolivian home. Most Bolivians live quite humbly.

Never arrive early or even on time, as it is considered very rude.

Always bring a gift for the host or hostess and their children (see "Gift-Giving Etiquette").

Bolivians love to converse, so be prepared to make plenty of small talk.

Do not leave directly after the meal is completed; instead, stick around and chat for a Although.

## *Whatever You Do...*

- Don't eat anything with your fingers; use utensils.
- Don't get up from the table until everyone has completed their meal.
- Don't accept the first offer of food from your host or hostess; instead, wait for that person to insist.
- Don't whisper to any one person when in a group.
- Don't think a telephone conversation is an acceptable substitute for meeting in person. You will rarely accomplish anything of value over the telephone.
- Don't ever underestimate the importance of friendships, business relationships, and personal referrals.
- Don't refer to yourself as an American, but rather as a North American.
- Don't assume negotiations are final until every detail is agreed upon. Until that point is reached, your Bolivian counterparts may attempt to renegotiate issues that were previously decided.

- Don't forget that major cities, such as La Paz, have very high altitudes. You may need to give your body time to adjust, so build this consideration into your travel schedule.

# Chapter 3

# Brazil

## 10 reasons people do business in Brazil

1. Brazil is South America's economic giant, rated tenth in the world.

2. Agriculturally, Brazil is the world's number one producer of coffee, oranges, and bananas, and a top exporter of sugar and soy beans.

3. On an industrial scale, Brazil is involved in automobile production, chemicals, textiles, plastics, and much more.

4. With the stabilization and growth of the Brazilian economy, demands for imports have increased, creating new business opportunities for U.S. exporters.

5. Business relationships are key to "turning the corporate wheel."

6. Top U.S. imports include computer software and accessories, equipment for pollution management, medical supplies, and gas/oil field equipment.

7. The mining of metal ores and manufacturing of related products are among Brazil's major industries.

8. Brazilian companies are typically looking for long-term investments and long-lasting business relationships.

9. The consumer population in Brazil is very accessible.

10. Corporate culture takes the cautious but faithful route.

The largest country in South America is also the fifth largest country in the world. The Republic of Brazil is a vast land covering more than 3.3 million square miles, nearly half of the continent, with 4,600 miles of coastline looking out to the Atlantic Ocean. Brazil borders every country in South America except for Chile and Ecuador. This huge nation is home to a variety of climates and natural attractions, including immense rainforests and the world's largest river, the Amazon. Add to this what are among the planet's richest and most extensive varieties of flora and fauna, as well as abundant natural resources, and you can understand why Brazil is a magnet for foreign investors and developers.

There are four primary geographic regions in Brazil: the long Atlantic seaboard region on the east coast; the Planalto Brasileiro (central plateau), a highlands area that covers a large portion of Brazil's interior; and two sections in the southeast called the Paraguay Basin and the Amazon Basin, the latter of which contains the Amazon Forest, where you will find 30 percent of the world's remaining forestland. Rio de Janeiro, on the southeastern coast, is Brazil's best-known city but is not, as many think, the country's capital. That honor belongs to Brasilia, located on a plateau in the central region. Sao Paulo is another well-known city, especially to businesspeople. Although the country is huge, the vast majority of the land is unsettled, with approximately 90 percent of its 158.7 million population occupying primarily urban areas.

Without question, Brazil is a true melting pot of nationalities. Unlike other South American countries, there is no Indian heritage here; the land was conquered in the 1500s by Portugal, which enslaved the natives in order to grow sugar cane and otherwise exploit the fertile lands. By the next century, African slaves were being brought in to work in the cane fields and gold mines, and by the early 1800s the country had become rich and strong enough to declare its independence from Portugal, establishing the Brazilian Empire.

By this time, coffee had become Brazil's primary export, and industrial powers brought about a coup in 1899 that led to a series of military supervised governments. This in turn led to the rise of Getúlio Vargas, a notorious fascist who dominated Brazilian politics for 30 years until he was overthrown in 1954.

Subsequent attempts to establish a democratic government were thwarted by rampant economic problems, political mismanagement, and fear of Communism. As a result, the military took over again in the early 1960s, and did not relinquish control until 1989, at which time the first free elections were held and Fernando Collar de Mello was elected president. In 1992, however, charges of corruption and economic mismanagement brought down de Mello's administration.

However, from November 1994 through today, Brazil has become reasonably stable under the leadership of President Fernando Cardoso, although it still suffers from a poor reputation stemming from the gross disparity between its economic classes and a high inflation rate.

Meanwhile, interracial unions, as well as a large influx of European immigrants, have given Brazil a cultural diversity unequaled by any other Latin American country. Many famous dances, including the samba, the bossa nova, and the lambada, originated here, and many famous writers, including Jorge Amado, have called the country home.

# Statistics and Information

### Air Travel

When flying to Brazil, you may land at the Sao Paolo Guarulhos International Airport or the smaller Congo Has Airport. In either case, taxis will be available to get you to your destination.

If you are planning to travel to Brazil during the months of December, February, and July, be sure to schedule your flights far in advance, as these are very busy months.

### Country Codes

Brazil's country code is 55.

City codes:

- 11 for Sao Paolo.
- 61 for Brasilia.

### Currency

Brazil's currency is called the *real*, which is available in denominations of 500,100, 50, 10, 5 and 1. One *real* is equivalent to 100 centavos.

Bureaus called *cambios* can be found throughout the country and are ideal places to exchange both cash and travelers' checks. You should also have no problem using major credit cards anywhere in Brazil.

### Dates

Just as in other Latin American countries, dates are written by listing the day of the week first, followed by the number of the month and then the year. For instance, March 5, 2010 would be listed as 5/3/10. When writing this date in longhand, the appropriate form is el cinco de marzo de 2010.

## *Ethnic Makeup*

With a population nearing 167 million, Brazil is overflowing with ethnicity and diversity. More than half of Brazilians are of European descent, although the remainder consists of mulattos, African Americans, mestizos, Japanese, and a mix of many other nationalities.

## *Holidays and Religious Celebrations*

| | |
|---|---|
| January 1 | New Year's Day |
| January 20 | St. Sebastian Day (celebrated in Rio) |
| January 25 | Foundation of the City (celebrated in Sao Paulo) |
| February/March | Carnival Celebration and Festivities |
| March/April | Good Friday and Easter |
| April 21 | Tiradentes' Day |
| May 1 | Labor Day |
| June (variable) | Corpus Christi |
| September 7 | Independence Day |
| October 12 | Day Our Lady Appeared |
| November 2 | All Souls' Day |
| November 15 | Proclamation of the Republic |
| December 25 | Christmas |

Be sure to avoid scheduling appointments around these holidays, when the majority of businesses close to allow employees to be with their families and take part in festivities.

If the date of a holiday happens to fall in the middle of the work week, it is typically celebrated on a Monday or Friday instead. However, there are some exceptions to this rule. *Note:* It is not uncommon for some businesses to close when the Brazilian soccer team is playing significant games.

## Language

The official language in Brazil is Portuguese. Spanish is understood by many Brazilians, but it is not commonly spoken.

Numerous people in the Brazilian business world speak English, so you can expect the majority of top executives and other important individuals to be reasonably fluent.

## Religion

About 72 percent of Brazilians are Roman Catholic, 21 percent are Protestant, and 1 percent are atheist. The remainder are a mixture of New Age religions and spiritual movements.

## Time Zone Differences

Brazil is about the size of the United States, making it large enough to be divided into time zones. The majority of Brazil is:

- Three hours behind Greenwich Mean Time.
- Two hours ahead Eastern Standard Time.

Western Brazil is:

- Four hours behind Greenwich Mean Time.
- One hour ahead of Eastern Standard Time.

## Weather

In the highland areas of Brazil, such as Sao Paulo, moderate temperatures are common. However, the major section of the country sports a tropical to subtropical climate. The southern portion of the country is the only area that experiences extreme climate changes from one season to the next. Note that Rio de Janeiro is especially hot and humid in the summer months of December to February.

It is important to remember that when it rains in Brazil, it usually pours, so be prepared with umbrella and raincoat, especially if you are in the Amazon Basin.

# Etiquette

## *Business Attire*

As it is in Rome, when in Brazil, do as the Brazilians do. A high value is placed on an individual's wardrobe in this country. Men should wear suits of dark colors such as black, charcoal, or navy, complemented by a high-quality conservative tie. Keep your shoes polished and well maintained. Take note of what your Brazilian counterparts are wearing. Upper-level executives may be seen wearing a three-piece suit, whereas lower-level employees typically wear two-piece suits.

Women should dress in a feminine manner and with flare; avoid wearing anything that could be considered masculine. Dresses, suits, pantsuits, skirts, and blouses are the norm. Brazilians notice details, so be sure to wear well-applied makeup and keep your nails nice and manicured.

When entertaining or being entertained (whether in a restaurant or in someone's home), dark suits for men and elegant dresses or skirts and blouses for women are the norm.

Try to avoid wearing combinations of yellow and green, which are the colors found in the Brazilian flag. If you wear an outfit containing these colors, you may be mocked.

When walking the streets or shopping, be sure to dress fashionably. Men should wear slacks or khakis and a quality long-sleeved shirt; women should wear slacks or a skirt. Avoid wearing tennis shoes or shorts in public.

## *Business Card Etiquette*

Be sure to bring plenty of business cards with you. Although it is not necessary, it would be wise to have your card printed in Portuguese on the opposite side. If you are unable to do this ahead of time, printing and stationery shops in Brazil can usually translate your card within 24 hours.

## Business Entertaining/Dining

Business entertaining typically is done during lunches and dinners; meeting for breakfast is rare and undesirable. Set aside at least two hours for a business lunch, and no less than three for a business dinner. You should arrive promptly for your business meal, but don't be surprised if you have to wait.

If you are the host, be sure to entertain your guest at only the best restaurants; this will add positively to your image and that of your company. Brush up on your basic table manners. Brazilians consider themselves sophisticated people and abide by rules of etiquette when dining.

Engage in small talk and social pleasantries until your host initiates business—or, if you are the host, until the time seems right to begin. Keep in mind that your Brazilian contacts place great significance on relationships. A common criticism concerning North Americans is that they tend to "jump right into business" before a relationship has been formed. Be sure you communicate that people and relationships take priority over business; if you don't, you can kiss your Brazilian investments good-bye.

By the same token, don't expect a lot of discussion during the meal. Brazilians often choose to concentrate on their enjoyment of the meal, and leave conversation for when the eating has been completed.

*Table manners:* Cut all foods with your knife; never use your fork to cut, even if the food is very tender. After you have cut your food, carefully position your knife so that the tip of the blade is resting on the plate and the handle is lying on the table. Then use your fork to eat. Be sure not to touch food with your fingers, Because Brazilians consider this rude. Make a point of eating everything with silverware, including fruit and sandwiches.

To indicate that you have completed your meal, place your knife and fork horizontally across your plate with your fork tines up.

Some special Brazilian dishes that you may encounter include a popular treat called *acarajé,* which is often sold on street corners. This consists of fried beans mashed and shaped into balls stuffed with seafood and spices. You also may eat a bean and meat stew called *feijoada*; *carurur,* a mixture of shrimp, onions, peppers, okra, and other vegetables; and *moqueca,* a tasty seafood stew.

## Conversation

Brazilians are fast talkers and enthusiastic conversationalists, so expect loud, fast-paced conversation. It is important that you mimic the enthusiasm of your counterparts. If you don't, they may assume that you are cold and unfriendly.

Use steady eye contact when conversing with your Brazilian colleagues; it is considered a great insult to break eye contact.

Expect your Brazilian counterpart to stand in close proximity to you although talking. Frequent touching and hand motions are also the norm when conversing.

You can expect to be interrupted often during conversations with Brazilians. Don't be offended you are "cut off" or if the person you're talking to interjects confrontational statements. This is simply a way of displaying interest and enthusiasm for the subject under discussion.

Good topics of conversation include sports such as soccer, basketball, fishing, skiing, horse racing, and volleyball; Brazilian dances; good tourist sights; food; the importance of family; vacationing; and positive aspects of Brazil's industry.

The people of Brazil enjoy conversation that "goes with the flow." As a result, you should avoid dominating the conversation or attempting to direct it.

Be aware that Brazilians consider their personal lives (such as family, salary, professional status) to be very private topics of conversation. Whatever you do, be sure not to probe. However, don't take offense if you are asked personal questions dealing with your salary, religion, marital status, etc. Keep your cool and respond in a manner that maintains your privacy, slowly changing the subject being discussed. For example, if asked how much you make annually, you could respond by saying, "Oh, I can't complain; my employer treats me well. The thing that I've discovered, however, is that money isn't everything. Family, friends, and a well-balanced life hold far greater value to me."

Topics of conversation to avoid include politics, religion, ethnic and class differences, and economic difficulties. Never say anything negative concerning Brazil (for example, its government, cities, food, sports, history, etc.).

## Gestures and Public Manners

Do not make the North American sign for "okay" (thumb and index finger together) in Brazil, as this gesture will be perceived as vulgar.

One gesture you can use involves scraping your fingers underneath your chin, which communicates "I don't know" or "I don't understand." This is sometimes used when responding to a question. In addition, snapping your fingers although speaking or listening gives emphasis to what has been said.

When Brazilians see something pleasurable, they use their hands as a telescope to indicate they like what they see. Pulling at one's earlobe is another sign of appreciation.

To beckon someone, simply extend your hand (palm down) and make a scratching motion with your fingers.

Take care with cigarettes; smoking is illegal in public places, including restaurants.

Don't shove or bump anyone when standing in a line or in crowds, even if you feel others pushing you.

## Gift-Giving Etiquette

It is not required that you provide a gift upon an initial meeting with your Brazilian contact. However, once a relationship has been established, a gift would be in order, such as pocket radios, portable CD players, calculators, small electronic planners, address books, quality notebooks, nice pens, music, artwork, whiskey, or fine wines.

Do not give gifts that contain the colors black or purple as these are colors of mourning, and similarly, do not give handkerchiefs.

Avoid giving anything with a sharp edge (knives, letter openers, scissors, etc.). Such objects represent the severing of relationships to Brazilians.

Don't give practical gifts or things that may be perceived as too personal—for example, a tie, a wallet, jewelry, perfume, key chain, sunglasses, etc. In addition, avoid giving anything that is too expensive. Your Brazilian counterpart may be embarrassed by the generosity or assume the gift is a bribe.

Refrain from presenting gifts when business is not being discussed; instead, wait until the meeting has ended. Social settings provide the most ideal times to present a gift.

### Greetings and Introductions

Greetings and introductions play an important role in Brazilian business relationships. You can expect your initial introductions to be warm, loud, and exciting occasions. How you greet your Brazilian counterparts in return will play an important part in developing first impressions and continuing relationships.

Be sure to shake hands with everyone present, both when arriving and departing from an event. If you know the rank of your Brazilian colleagues, attempt to acknowledge them by rank from highest to lowest. Expect a warm and extended handshake; physical touching is also the norm (shoulder patting, kissing, hugging, etc.). Avoid restraining or tightening up if you are offered one of these affectionate gestures; to do so may be perceived as an insult. Note that as the relationship with your Brazilian counterparts grows, the level of affection will also increase. Always maintain good, steady eye contact when shaking hands and when making small talk.

Women typically kiss on both cheeks when meeting and departing. If a woman is married she receives two kisses, one on each cheek. If the woman is single however, she receives a total of three kisses (for example, left cheek, right cheek, left cheek).

Recognition and status are important in Brazil; therefore titles should be used with surnames whenever appropriate—i.e., Doctor Santiago, President García, Executive Sánchez. However, be aware that some individuals may introduce themselves by using their title with their first name, and may, in fact, prefer to be addressed this way. If an individual does not have a title, he or she may be addressed by using pleasantries such as Mr. (*Señor*) or Mrs. (*Señora*) followed by the person's surname. It is always a good idea to ask people how they prefer to be addressed.

In Brazil, individuals usually have two surnames. When written, the mother's surname comes before the father's surname—for example, *Juan Valdez Mantilla*. It is appropriate, however, to address people using their father's surname—for example, *Señor Mantilla*.

When a women marries, she usually takes her husband's surname. For business purposes, however, it is common for women to use their father's surname.

In Brazil, people quickly move to a first name basis. However, never refer to an individual using his or her first name until invited to do so.

### *Hierarchy Is Important*

Pecking order is important in Brazil. For that reason, it should be easy to determine who will be making the ultimate decision if you key into the highest-ranking person at your meetings. This is why knowing the titles of the people attending your meeting is important, as it will help you to identify the top decision-maker.

## How Decisions Are Made

Unlike those in other Latin American countries, Brazilians do not attempt to apply universal truths to every new circumstance. Instead, they approach each situation in an intuitive and analytical manner, dealing with it as its own entity. This approach has a direct effect on the decision-making process.

Brazilians also place a significant amount of emphasis on feelings; although situations are dealt with analytically, emotional responses greatly influence decisions. Therefore, if your company wants to do business with a company in Brazil, you should realize that facts, charts, graphs, and the "right sell" are not going to cut it if your cross-cultural colleagues do not feel good about the relationship. For this reason, the ability to form personal relationships, practice proper etiquette, and maintain cultural sensitivity are key factors to doing business in Brazil.

## Meeting Manners

It is important to remember that in doing business, Brazilians place a lot of emphasis on the personal relationship they are able to develop with a company's representative. Thus, when determining who will be representing your company in Brazil, what that person knows will not be nearly as important as the way he packages himself or the charisma he possesses. These qualities can, in fact, make or break the relationship.

It is also important to maintain continuity by sending the same person, whether it is you or someone else, to meetings. Failure to do so may slow down or even damage business relations. Establishing a cross-cultural relationship may take many trips and meetings, so if you are not in it for the long haul, you shouldn't be in it at all.

Be sure to schedule meetings at least two to three weeks in advance. The most effective way to do this is over the telephone. Always confirm the appointment in writing, preferably via e-mail or fax. The best times for meetings in Brazil are between 10 a.m. and noon, and 3 p.m. and 5 p.m. Early meetings usually make for a relaxed environment, allowing both parties to focus on the issues at hand.

Expect initial meetings with Brazilian associates to be somewhat formal. As the relationship grows, the atmosphere of the meetings will change accordingly.

Always engage in small talk before and after discussing business. This will let your colleagues know that your relationship with them takes priority over business. In addition, never leave as soon as the meeting is over; this will insult your colleagues and communicate that you have to be somewhere more important.

With the exception of Sao Paulo's residents, the majority of Brazilians conduct meetings in a slow-paced, casual environment. Sao Paulo business people, however, tend to mimic the European style of conducting more formal business meetings.

Private offices are not as common in Brazil as they are in the United States. You can expect that many individuals are required to share office space—even senior executives. This situation may consequently lead to a number of interruptions throughout the course of your meeting. Prepare yourself beforehand for any inconveniences in order to remain patient.

Due to their emphasis on building relationships, you can expect negotiations with your Brazilian counterparts to require several face-to-face meetings over an extended period of time. Remember, it takes time to establish the trust necessary to develop a successful business relationship. In addition, power and prestige are typically more important negotiating tools than money in Brazil. Keep this in mind during the negotiation process.

When making a presentation, visual aids will be very valuable in making your point. Be sure to have all documents translated into Portuguese; this should be done before your arrival in Brazil. Also plan for an intermediary or local agent to assist with some of the bureaucracy you will encounter.

Do not expect documents to be signed immediately after an agreement is reached; a handshake and a person's word is considered to be sufficient to seal a deal. Documents are prepared and signed by attorneys later. Be aware that in various cultures, the conditions of signed agreements are not perceived as binding. Therefore, once you've signed a contract with Brazilian counterparts, the terms may still be subject to change.

## *Punctuality*

It would be easy to assume Brazilians are lazy or "slackers" due to their poor punctuality habits. This may provide the biggest stumbling block for North Americans in their desire to deal with their Brazilian counterparts. Despite this, you should plan to be on time for all meetings, even if others may be late. In expectation that you may be waiting, bring some material to read or work to do. Note that people of a higher rank are more likely to keep you waiting.

Do not arrange back-to-back meetings. Instead, give yourself two to three hours between each.

Never be late for a business meal or meeting at a restaurant; typically, Brazilians are punctual under those circumstances.

Above all, be patient. Don't make the mistake of thinking you can change 500 years of culture; it will never happen! Business in Brazil will require long-term investments of time, money, and patience. If you can't conform to Brazilian culture, you shouldn't be doing business there.

## *Seating Etiquette*

In a business setting, your Brazilian contact will probably sit at the head of the table, and you will be offered the seat to the immediate right of that person. When you are the host, give the most important seat (at the head of the table) to your highest-ranking Brazilian contact.

### Tipping Tips

Restaurants typically include a 10 percent gratuity charge in their bills. Patrons often leave an additional 5 percent tip if they enjoyed the service.

Tip taxi drivers 10 percent of the fare. Be sure to ask the price of a ride before getting into the car; in most cases, Brazilian taxis have set prices.

Porters should be tipped about $1 per bag.

### Toasting Etiquette

When you are toasted, be sure to raise your goblet and propose a toast in return to your Brazilian host.

### When You Are Invited to a Home

You should always consider it an honor to be invited to a Brazilian's home. It is appropriate to bring a gift such as candy, fine chocolates, wine, scotch, or flowers. It is also a nice gesture to bring games or candy as gifts for any children in the house.

You should plan on arriving about 30 minutes late if you are invited to dinner and 45 minutes to an hour late if you're invited to a party.

After being entertained at someone's home, it is good etiquette to send the hostess flowers and a thank-you note the following day.

### Women in Business

If any group of women in Latin America is "liberated," it is Brazilian women, who have made great strides in the business arena. For this reason, professional women from abroad can expect to have little trouble dealing with male colleagues in Brazil.

## Whatever You Do...

- Don't mispronounce or misspell the name of your Brazilian colleague. Such a mistake will be interpreted as a grave insult.

- Don't refer to Brazilians as "latinos" or "Latin Americans."

- Don't use phrases like "In America we..." or "As an American, I..." Remember, Brazilians also refer to themselves as Americans.

- Don't attempt to rush negotiations when dealing with Brazilian counterparts; be patient and allow the situation to develop slowly.

- Don't forget to address your Brazilian contact by title.

- Don't assume that all Latin Americans want to be addressed by their last names. It is actually considered appropriate for individuals to address high-ranking women or older women with "Doña" followed by their first name.

# Chapter 4

# Chile

---

**10 reasons people do business in Chile**

1. Chile's economy is "booming" thanks to such major industries as copper mining and winemaking.

2. Chileans observe strict business ethics.

3. Compared to other Latin American countries, Chile has little bureaucracy, so business negotiations move along at a faster pace.

4. Chile has strong, positive relations with the United States.

5. Chilean companies will follow contract agreements to the letter.

6. Business-related conflicts in Chile are often quickly resolved.

7. Chile is a country known for producing world-renowned wines, literary masterpieces, and artistic movements.

8. Business in Chile is conducted in a formal and professional manner.

9. Chileans have a reputation for paying their debts on time.

10. Chile is known for its acceptance and encouragement of foreign investors; the government has passed numerous laws to ensure good business.

---

The Republic of Chile is a large, unique country that meanders along the entire bottom half of South America's western coast, providing some of the most diverse geographic sights of any country in the world. Over 2,600 miles long, at its widest point Chile is rarely more than 124 miles across. The Andes mountains are most responsible for Chile's narrow size, in effect separating it from its neighbors with the exception of Peru, which it touches in the north. Officially, it is bordered by Peru and Bolivia on the north and Argentina on the east, Although the Pacific Ocean lies on its west coast. Chile also shares control of the island territory of Tierra del Fuego (at the continent's tip) with Argentina and maintains full control of Easter Island and the territory of Juan Fernández, both of which lie well off the western coast.

The extreme length of the country can make Chile a fascinating place to visit. In fact, there are 12 distinct geographic regions in this country, from the desert areas of the north to the glacial scenery in the south. Tall mountains can give way to deep canyons, Although the coastline is punctuated with a myriad of beaches and inlets. The terrain and wildlife throughout the country offer a wide variety of beauty for visitors, and there are numerous national parks for millions of tourists to visit yearly. Chile's best-known city is its capital, Santiago, located in the central region, where the majority of the country's population of more than 14 million make their homes.

Chile has a democratic government led by the Christian Democrats. Like many South American countries, a large portion of its current population came about as a result of European immigration and consequent intermixing with the native populations. As a result, the vast majority of the population is mestizo. The heaviest European influence is Spanish, thanks to the conquistadors who invaded the country in the 1500s. By the early 1800s, Chileans had achieved independence and Bernardo O'Higgins became the nation's new leader.

At first, the country was much smaller than it is now, but it grew quickly thanks to territory seized from Peru and Bolivia. The following years saw relative stability and the occasional civil war, and by the mid-20th century, Chile had no real government to speak of, just a loose infrastructure in the ruling classes that swung between conservative and liberal elements.

However, instability set in during the 1970s, when Marxist Salvador Allende imposed his rule on the country, instituting a terrible time during which thousands of Chilean citizens "disappeared."

In 1973, Allende was overthrown by a military coup headed by General Pinochet. Although Pinochet succeeded in restoring economic stability to the country, Chilean voters rejected him and eventually elected the current president, Eduardo Frei, whose reforms made some headway in dealing with the country's drastic poverty levels.

Chile is probably best known for its vast and diverse landscapes, as well as its rich culture. Chilean intellectuals have often been globally influential on literature, art, architecture, and music. Its most famous native sons are Nobel prize winners Pablo Neruda and Gabriela Mistral.

# Statistics and Information

### Air Travel

One of Chile's most popular international airports is the Aeropuerto Internacional Arturo Merino Benitez. The airport is in the city of Pudahuel, which is located approximately 16 miles outside Santiago.

### Country Codes

Chile's country code is 56.

City codes:

- 2 for Santiago.
- 41 for Concepción.
- 32 for Valparaiso.

### Currency

Chile's unit of currency is called the *peso*. These bills circulate in denominations of 5,000, 1,000, 500, and 100. Chile's coins are *centavos* and are available in amounts of 100, 50, 5, 1. One peso equals 100 centavos. Money and travelers' checks can be exchanged at large hotels and money-exchange houses. Usually these establishments are faster than banks and offer the same or better rates. Credit cards can be used just about anywhere. Note that banks close at 2 p.m. in Chile.

### Dates

Chileans write their dates in the European style format of day, month, and year. For example: January 30, 1976 would be written 30.1.99. When writing this date in longhand or keying it on a computer, it would be written as el 30 de *enero* de 1976.

## Ethnic Makeup

Chile's population of more than 14 million people is 94 percent mestizo, 3 percent native Indian, and 3 percent European.

## Holidays and Religious Celebrations

| | |
|---|---|
| January 1 | New Year's Day |
| March/April | Good Friday and Easter Sunday |
| May 1 | Labor Day |
| May 21 | Battle of Iquique Commemoration |
| June 29 | Saints Day: Peter and Paul |
| August 15 | Feast of the Assumption |
| September 11 | Official Holiday |
| September 18 | Independence Day |
| September 19 | Day of the Army |
| October 12 | Columbus Day |
| November 1 | All Saints' Day |
| December 8 | Immaculate Conception |
| December 25 | Christmas |

Chileans often take vacations during the months of January and February (summer months in Chile). If possible, avoid scheduling appointments during this time.

## Language

The official language of Chile is Castellano Spanish. Chileans are known for speaking a very conservative and pure form of the Spanish dialect. Although a very small number of Indians live in the country, you occasionally may hear their native language, which is known as *Mapuche*.

Upper-level businesspeople and well-educated individuals should speak English, which can also be heard in tourist areas, hotels catering to business and leisure travelers, U.S.-based restaurant chains, and government establishments.

### Religion

Chile does not have an official religion. Approximately 74 percent of Chileans are Roman Catholic, Although 14 percent are Protestant, 1 percent Jewish, and the remaining 11 percent consist of atheists and followers of various religions.

### Time Zone Differences

Chile is:

- Four hours behind Greenwich Mean Time.
- One hour ahead of U.S. Eastern Standard Time.

### Weather

Due to its vast geography, Chile's climate varies throughout its many regions. Northern Chile features a tropical to subtropical climate, Although Central Chile is more moderate and seasonal, and southern Chile has arctic-like temperatures. What is important to remember is that this country's seasons are the reverse of what you are familiar with in the United States, with cooler temperatures experienced during the months of May to August.

# Etiquette

### Business Attire

When doing business in Chile it is better to dress in a formal, conservative manner, in keeping with preferred business attire practices. By dressing informally (for example, a sports coat, khakis, casual shoes), you will communicate a lack of respect for your Chilean counterpart.

Men should wear blue or gray suits, white shirts, and conservative ties. Women should wear blue or gray business suits and shoes with low heels. Both men and women should wear minimal, conservative jewelry or none at all. If you are observed wearing expensive-looking accessories, your Chilean counterparts may assume you are proud and absorbed in your own interests.

If invited to dinner at someone's home or to a restaurant, men should wear a suit and tie and women should wear an elegantly conservative dress.

Avoid wearing outfits that are extremely bright or anything that would attract attention. It is far better to err on the side of formality. By mirroring the business attire of your Chilean counterparts, you will provide them with a sense of comfort and security.

## Business Card Etiquette

Always bring plenty of business cards with you to Chile, and have Spanish translations printed on the opposite side of the card. Business cards should be exchanged shortly after the initial handshake.

Always keep these general rules in mind when exchanging business cards:

- Never fold, crease, or fiddle with a business card you have been given.
- Always take a few brief seconds to admire your associate's business card after it has been handed to you.
- When handed a business card, don't simply stick it in your pocket. Have a quality business card case with you and make a point of putting it in that.
- Never fling or toss your business card at your colleague; instead, present it with care.
- Always smile and make eye contact when presenting and receiving cards.

## Business Entertaining/Dining

Breakfast typically is eaten between 7 a.m. and 9 a.m. Lunch, the biggest meal of the day, consists of a two hour break somewhere between noon and 3 p.m. Dinner is served between 8 p.m. and 10 p.m. A small break, called *onces*, is taken between 5 p.m. and 6 p.m. *Onces* consists of tea, pastries, bite-sized sandwiches, and other snacks.

Be on your best behavior when dining in Chile. The Chileans emphasize good table manners and are sure to notice your eating habits (good or bad). Consequently, European-style table manners are a must!

Business entertaining is usually a social event. It is a great opportunity to engage in small talk and develop your relationship with your Chilean counterparts. Allow your host to initiate any discussion of business; if you're the host, restrain yourself from introducing business. It is important that you allow conversation to flow freely and for guests to enjoy each other's company. This will demonstrate for your Chilean colleagues that a relationship with them is of greater priority than company business. If you can't keep these priorities straight, you shouldn't be doing business in Chile.

*Table manners:* Always keep your hands above the table, and simply allow your wrist to rest on the edge; it is poor etiquette to keep your hands out of sight. Take small bites and chew slowly; it isn't your first meal and it won't be your last. Bear in mind that Chileans find chewing loudly, clanging silverware, scraping the plate, and "smacking your chops" to be detestable habits.

"Finger food" is nonexistent during formal meals; use the silverware provided. By the same token, never lick your fingers; it will mark you as a rude and unrefined person.

Don't reject outright anything you are served. If you don't care for the food, at least take a few bites to be polite.

## Conversation

Good topics of conversation in Chile include positive aspects of Chilean history and its economy, Chilean art and literature, wine and food, suggested tourist sights, Chile's landscape, overseas travel, and sports such as skiing and fishing. As in any country, avoid saying anything of a negative or derogatory nature about the country, its government, its cities, and its culture. Chileans are a very patriotic people and likely to take offense.

Other topics of conversation to avoid include politics, wars, surrounding countries such as Argentina, Bolivia and Peru, the Araucanian Indians, ethnic and social classes, and religion.

Do not continually talk about yourself. Instead, ask more questions than you answer and show a real interest in the other person. It is acceptable to ask simple questions about a person's family (for example, if they have children, how many, etc.), but don't probe. Most Latin Americans consider their home life very personal. Also, do not ask an individual about their vocation; allow the person to volunteer that information.

If you want to build rapport with Chilean counterparts, be sure to have a basic knowledge of the history and economy of Chile. Not only are these topics good areas of conversation, but your Chilean associates will appreciate your knowledge of their country.

When conversing with Chileans, do not take offense if you are interrupted. Chileans perceive interruptions as a means of participating in conversations and an indicator that the discussion is interesting.

Expect people to stand in very close proximity Although conversing. Try not to back away when this happens. In addition to possibly hurting your Chilean counterpart, it may also inadvertently cause the person to move in closer.

## Gestures and Public Manners

There are numerous gestures that you should make a point of avoiding whenever you are in Chile. These include:

- Opening your palm and spreading your fingers; this communicates that someone or something is stupid.

- Raising a clenched fist over your head; this is perceived as a communist symbol.

- Pounding your fist into an open palm; this is a vulgar gesture in Chile.

- Flicking your fingers under your chin; this is interpreted as "I don't know" or "I don't care."

You should also avoid any behavior that may be interpreted as aggressive. Although Chileans are an animated people, using any sort of aggression will only portray you as rude.

Public respect is very important to Chileans. As a result, never do anything that will harm another person or cause an individual to lose face.

It is proper etiquette to always offer a cigarette to those in your group before smoking one yourself.

Always put your hand over your mouth when sneezing, coughing, yawning, etc.

Never use your index finger to point out another person or when calling someone to you; use your entire hand to do this instead.

### *Gift-Giving Etiquette*

If possible, it's always a good idea to familiarize yourself with the person to whom you want to present a gift. You can question this person's secretary or colleagues or simply gather information through small talk over the phone. Did he go to college or travel overseas? Does she have any hobbies? Such information will aid you in choosing the monetary level of the gift, as well as the type of gift. For example, you wouldn't give a very refined individual a Yankees baseball cap or a company T-shirt. Good gifts include North American crafts native to your region, liquor, quality candy, fine chocolates, a nice pen, fine cigarette lighters, a desk clock, or other accessories for an office.

Wait for the appropriate time to present your gift. If you expect to visit the person's home during your visit or if you will be meeting in a more formal setting, then refrain from presenting your gift at the airport or in a restaurant.

Be sure to wrap your gift and include a short note or card. This will communicate a deeper level of sincerity than just handing the person an item with your business card stuck to it.

Avoid giving any purple or black flowers, as they symbolize death and mourning.

Don't give a gift that is relatively expensive or too personal until you have developed a relationship with your Chilean counterpart; otherwise, the person receiving the present may consider it a bribe or feel you are being eccentric. Allow the depth of the relationship to set the tone for gift-giving. Note that once you have built a relationship with this person, it is always a plus to include university T-shirts, games, sports caps, flowers, etc., for the immediate family.

If you receive a gift from a Chilean, chances are you will be expected to open it immediately. Be gracious at all times, and be sure to send a thank-you note afterward; this is good etiquette that will strengthen your relationship with your Chilean counterpart.

### Greetings and Introductions

On the whole, Chileans are a warm and affectionate people. Greetings are typically a joyous occasion involving lots of physical touching. Your Chilean counterpart may seem somewhat formal during the initial meeting, but the warmth will increase with each successive encounter.

Greet your Chilean counterpart with a sincere and inviting handshake, accompanied by a smile and good eye contact, which is very important. Be sure to acknowledge all who are present by shaking hands. Be aware that a group "hello" is often perceived as rude and impersonal. Note that as friendships grow, handshakes are often followed by kissing, hugging, and backpatting. It is very important to mirror your Chilean counterparts' enthusiasm in these situations; if you don't, they may be offended.

Women kiss on both cheeks as a form of greeting. They don't actually touch lips to cheek, but administer mock kisses by quickly touching cheek to cheek and kissing the air.

*Names and titles:* An individual can be addressed by using the titles Mr. (*Señor*), Mrs. (*Señora*), or Miss (*Señorita*) followed by the person's surname. People can also be addressed by combining their professional titles with their surname; for example, Doctor Santiago, President García, or Executive Sánchez. However, the use of professional titles is less common in Chile than in the rest of Latin America. Thus, to be on the safe side, you may want to ask the person how they prefer to be addressed.

Be aware that the majority of Hispanics carry both their mother's and their father's surnames. The father's surname is listed first and would be used to address the individual. For example, *Carlos López García* would be addressed as *Señor López*.

When a women marries, she typically takes her husband's surname. However, she may choose to keep her father's surname for her professional identity.

### Hierarchy Is Important

There is a definite hierarchical order in Chilean businesses. For that reason, when scheduling meetings and also when greeting others, be sure to defer to the most senior person present. If you are in a situation where you don't know who this person is, you may be able to determine it by identifying who commands the most presence or is clearly being deferred to.

### How Decisions Are Made

The business culture of Chile is less bureaucratic than other Latin American countries, and upper-level executives are known for their efficiency. Therefore, negotiations and business transactions move at a faster pace. Contract agreements are followed rigidly, problems are resolved quickly, and payments are made as scheduled. Decisions are made by those who are clearly in authority. Attempts have been made to incorporate group consensus decision making, but overall the power still belongs to the few at the top.

### Meeting Manners

Appointments should be scheduled at least two or three weeks in advance. Always confirm your appointment before your visit to Chile and upon your arrival in the country. The most ideal times to schedule appointments with your Chilean counterparts are from 10 a.m. to 12:30 p.m. and 3 p.m. to 5 p.m. It is not uncommon for individuals to meet sometime between 11 a.m. and 3 p.m., combining their meeting with a business lunch.

Of all the Latin American countries engaged in business with others, Chile is one of the most efficient and least bureaucratic. However, business will still move at a slower pace than what you may be used to in European or North American countries. This is partly because Chileans have a relatively conservative mindset and business ethics are taken very seriously.

### Punctuality

Chileans are typically more punctual than other Latin Americans, but you should still expect your counterparts to be approximately 15 to 30 minutes late. As a foreign visitor, however, you will still be expected to arrive on time for all business and restaurant meetings. The exception to this is when you are invited to someone's home, in which case it is best to arrive approximately 15 minutes late. When you are invited to a party, it is appropriate to arrive at least 30 minutes late.

### Seating Etiquette

As it is in most Latin American countries, either the host or the most senior man will be seated at the head of the table, and the seat of honor will be to his immediate right. The second seat of honor will be to the immediate right of either the hostess or the second Chilean person in command.

### Tipping Tips

Depending on where you choose to dine, a gratuity will most likely be included in the bill. If you found the service pleasing, it is polite to leave an additional 5 percent tip on the table. If a gratuity is not included in your bill, then leave between 10 percent and 15 percent for a tip.

Porters should be tipped $1 for each piece of luggage.

It is not necessary to tip taxi drivers.

### Toasting Etiquette

When your Chilean contact proposes a toast to you, be sure to reciprocate by proposing one in return, punctuated by a "Salud!" or "Cheers!"

### When You Are Invited to a Home

It is considered good manners to arrive about 15 minutes late when invited to an individual's home. Be both gracious and appreciative.

It is a nice gesture to bring small gifts for children when invited to a home (games, candy, university T-shirts, etc.). Flowers or candy make nice gifts for the hostess. Don't bring things that are easily accessible in Chile; instead, provide U.S. games and candy.

If you are honored enough to be invited to someone's home, sending flowers and a thank-you note the following day is an appropriate way to express your gratitude.

## Whatever You Do...

- Don't ever underestimate the power of a Chilean secretary. If you want to get to a decision maker, it's always necessary to go through the "gate keeper" first.

- Don't attempt to bribe your Chilean business associates. Although this is acceptable in other Latin American countries, in Chile it could land you in jail.

- Don't use an aggressive approach when negotiating. Instead, slowly work on building good relationships in order to patiently make the transition to the business at hand.

- Don't be surprised if you see Italian, Chinese, and even Mexican restaurants in Chile; Chileans like diversity.

- Don't forget to tip an usher for helping you to your reserved seat when you go to the theatre.

- Don't forget to tip the postal carrier for delivering a letter for you. The person will expect a few pesos per piece of mail delivered.

# Chapter 5

# Colombia

## 8 reasons people do business in Colombia

1. Colombia is a country with a stable and growing economy.

2. Colombian companies are committed to long-term investments.

3. Colombia's key location on the Caribbean coast provides advantageous business opportunities.

4. U.S. products and brand names are very popular, due in large part to the good business relations that Colombia has established with the United States.

5. The people of Colombia have learned to adapt, cope, and prosper under political and social turmoil, which to many makes them attractive business partners.

6. Foreign visitors to Colombia are treated with great hospitality.

7. Colombia has a good and effective telecommunications system.

8. The government is a democracy that has achieved a measure of domestic tranquility despite numerous upheavals and challenges over the years.

The fourth-largest nation on the South American continent, the Republic of Colombia also has the distinction of being the only country on the continent to have coastlines on two major bodies of water: the Caribbean on the north and the Pacific Ocean on the west. Panama comes between, bordering Colombia at its northwest corner. Other countries that border Colombia include Venezuela on the east, Brazil on the southeast, Peru on the south, and Ecuador on the southwest. Large parts of the country are mountainous, with the Cordillera de los Andes splitting into three separate ranges that shelter two major valleys within Colombia's borders. Other distinctive geographical features include the Sierra Nevada de Santa Marta, the world's highest coastal mountain range, as well as the northeast deserts and the Pacific coast jungle.

Colombia lays claim to more species of animal and plant life than any other country in the world; this includes a record number of more than 1,550 species of birds. As a result of its immense biological diversity, the country harbors a large number of national parks and sanctuaries dedicated to preserving Colombian land and wildlife.

Colombia's capital is Bogotá, which is located on a large plateau in the central portion of the country. The majority of the country's population reside in the western half of the country, the Cordillera Central. Evidence of ancient civilizations still exist throughout Colombia, but its past has largely been uprooted by the heavy influx of European blood and cultures, resulting in a large percentage of mestizo. The primary European influence is Spanish; Spain monopolized Colombia for almost three centuries, and independence was not achieved until Simon Bolívar liberated the country in 1819. For about 10 years, Colombia existed in an uncertain alliance with Ecuador and Venezuela.

Civil and political differences between conservative and liberal elements of the population eventually led to numerous insurrections and civil wars and, ultimately, the War of a Thousand Days in 1899, a gruesome confrontation that yielded a tremendous loss of life. The turmoil continued on an even larger scale when the bloody civil war known as La Violenca began in 1948. This conflict between liberal and conservative factions continued until 1953, when a military coup brought an end to the fighting that had so long divided the country. In 1957, the two sides finally agreed to share power as the National Front. This arrangement formally ended in 1974, and the two-party system continues to this day, albeit with frequent challenges from radical groups attempting to undermine the government.

On the down side, Colombia has acquired a negative reputation because of the notorious drug cartels that operate within its borders. However, its positive aspects are what keep tourists and businesspeople returning to this country year after year. These aspects include Colombia's beautiful scenery and a very rich culture that is amply represented by native crafts, music, and literature; for example, Colombia's best-known native son is world-renowned novelist Gabriel García Márquez.

# Statistics and Information

### Air Travel

The Tobias Bolanos Airport is located about four miles outside San Jose. The Daniel Oduber International Airport is located approximately three to four miles outside Liberia in Gaunacaste.

## Country Codes

Colombia's country code is 57.

City codes:

- 1 for Bogota.
- 4 for Medellin.
- 2 for Cali.

## Currency

The unit of currency in Colombia is the *peso*. Bills circulate in denominations of 1,000, 500, 200, 100, 50, 20, 10, 5, and 1. Coins are found in peso denominations of 20, 10, 5, and 1, as well as 50 centavos.

Only certain banks will change money or cash travelers' checks, and of those, there may be only certain times when this can be done. The best way to get pesos in Colombia is to use your Visa or MasterCard at an automated teller machine that accepts them.

## Dates

Colombians write their dates in the European standard format of day/month/year. For example, January 30, 1999 would be written as 30/1/99. If this date were being written in a formal letter, it would be presented as "el 30 de *enero* de 1999."

## Ethnic Makeup

Colombia's population exceeds 36 million. Of this number, 58 percent are mestizo, 20 percent are of European descent, 14 percent are mulatto, 4 percent of African descent, and 3 percent are an African-Amerindian mix, although approximately 1 percent are indigenous Indian.

## Holidays and Religious Celebrations

January 1      New Year's Day

| | |
|---|---|
| January 6 | Epiphany |
| March 19 | Saint Joseph's Day |
| March/April | Good Friday and Easter Sunday |
| May 1 | Labor Day |
| June 19 | Feast of the Sacred Heart |
| June 29 | Saints Day: Peter & Paul |
| July 20 | Independence Day |
| August 7 | Battle of Boyaca |
| August 15 | Feast of the Assumption |
| October 12 | Columbus Day |
| November 1 | All Saints' Day |
| November 11 | The Independence of Cartagena |
| December 8 | Immaculate Conception |
| December 25 | Christmas |

When planning meetings, note that it is common for most Colombians to take their vacations during the months of December and January, and sometimes during June and July.

Do not plan parties or any festive events on November 1, All Saints Day. This is considered to be a day of mourning and remembrance for those who have passed away.

## Language

Spanish, often referred to as *castellano*, is the official language of Colombia. Upper-level executives and some government officials may speak English, but overall it is not widely spoken. There are as many as 75 Indian languages still in use throughout the country.

## Religion

Colombia does not have an official religion. About 95 percent of Colombians are Roman Catholic and the remaining 5 percent is a mix of different beliefs. In recent years, many have started to turn to Protestant faiths, and pockets of Mormons have begun to emerge.

## Time Zone Differences

Colombia is:

- Five hours behind Greenwich Mean Time.
- The same as U.S. Eastern Standard Time.

## Weather

Due to its diverse geography, Colombia's temperatures can range from tropical to subarctic. However, each region generally maintains consistent temperatures throughout the year. To determine what to pack for your trip, check the climate of your specific destination beforehand.

# Etiquette

## Business Attire

Mark Twain once said, "Clothes make the man. Naked people have little or no influence in society." He must have been Colombian in a past life! You can certainly bet that your Colombian associates will notice the way in which you are dressed and judge you accordingly. Colombians view a person's dress as an indicator of status. Be sure to dress conservatively, but with class. Make sure your clothes aren't outdated. It is definitely advisable to have all your business attire dry-cleaned and pressed before your visit to Colombia.

Men should wear dark-colored suits, white shirts, conservative ties, and dress shoes. Women should wear business suits and conservative but attractive dresses.

Colombians pay attention to detail. Wear good quality shoes that have been well kept and polished. Make sure your shoes are in style—no matter how good they look, shoes from the 1950s don't count! *Note:* Colombians only wear tennis shoes when engaged in aerobic activity.

Good hygiene is very important. Men's hair should be clean cut and above the collar. Women should be well groomed and appear professional at all times.

Check beforehand on the appropriate business attire for your specific destination. It is possible that warmer regions in Colombia may allow less formal attire.

### Business Card Etiquette

Bring a significant number of business cards when doing business in Colombia. It's always better to have too many than not enough.

Have your card printed in Spanish on the opposite side; this will be greatly appreciated. When presenting your business card, pass it to your counterpart with the Spanish side facing up and in such a way that he or she can read it without having to turn it around.

### Business Entertaining/Dining

Breakfast is typically a small meal and eaten at different times, depending on an individual's schedule. It is common for Colombians to eat their breakfast on the job.

Colombians break for lunch somewhere between 12:30 and 2:30 p.m. Lunch is the most important meal of the day and is usually eaten with one's family. Typically there is an hour break for coffee and conversation somewhere between 4 p.m. and 6 p.m. In most cases, dinner is enjoyed between 7 p.m. and 8:30 p.m.

Business entertaining is usually done over lunch and dinner. Entertaining is a great way to develop a personal relationship with your Colombian counterpart. Note that Colombians place great emphasis on getting to know a person before business is even conducted. As a result, it is important to wait for your Colombian counterpart to initiate any business conversation. This may take a although, however. Although it is customary for North Americans to cordially begin with small talk until they reach a point where it is time to "get down to business," Colombians are more likely to make the transition into business in a much more gradual manner. In fact, you may meet with your Colombian associate a number of times without ever discussing business. Be patient; the time will come when your contacts will feel they know you well enough to begin.

As Austin Powers would say, "Oh, behave!" Colombians are very formal, placing great value on proper table manners. Thus, when dining with your Colombian counterparts, be on your best behavior and observe all the appropriate rules of etiquette.

Always allow your host to take the lead. For example, wait to be instructed on where you should sit and never begin eating until everyone is served and the host starts to eat. Be sociable, but allow your host to direct the flow of conversation.

*Table Manners:* Never help yourself to food without offering it to the other members of your party first. Also use the appropriate utensils at all times; regardless of how tempting it may be, avoid touching food with your hands. Above all, don't chew with your mouth open or attempt to talk with a mouthful of food.

Always try the food you are offered; even if you don't care for the cuisine, it is polite to take a few bites.

As you enjoy the meal, keep in mind that you are being entertained, not preparing for hibernation. Your Colombian counterparts will notice if you are a glutton, so always leave some food on your plate to show you have been satisfied.

When you have finished eating, place your utensils horizontally across your plate. This will let others know that you have finished eating.

## Conversation

Familiarize yourself with Colombian history and culture before your visit. Having a basic knowledge of these things will open doors to conversation and help to establish common ground. Note that Colombians are very proud of their culture and national accomplishments. Never say anything negative concerning Colombia; always focus on the positive.

Good topics of conversation include: Colombian history, literature, art, music, coffee, and cuisine, as well as the city you are visiting, Colombia's diverse landscape, and the region of the U.S. from where you hail.

Topics of conversations to avoid include politics, terrorism, religion, illegal drugs and drug cartels, and any negative remarks concerning bullfighting.

## Gestures and Public Manners

Be sure to use good eye contact when conversing with a Colombian. If you don't, it will be taken as an insult.

Pushing is very common when standing in lines or crowds. You need to be assertive in order to reach your destination. However, don't engage in pushing matches.

Always cover your mouth when yawning, sneezing, coughing, etc.

As in other Latin American countries, there are certain gestures that have specific meanings in Colombia. For instance, moving the edge of one hand back and forth across the back of your opposite hand indicates a business agreement to share profits, although hitting your hand against your elbow may indicate that you are labeling a person "cheap" or "selfish."

In order to demonstrate the height of an animal or object, Colombians extend their hand down and hold it at the appropriate level. To indicate a human's height, they extend the hand palm out and thumb up. To show how long something is, Colombians extend their right arm and mark the appropriate length with their left hand.

Making the North American gesture for "okay" and placing it over the nose is one way that Colombians will reference a homosexual.

Never point to someone or use your index finger to beckon. Instead, extend your hand palm down and use your fingers to motion toward yourself.

### Gift-Giving Etiquette

In a business situation, good gifts to present include nice pens, office accessories, and gifts native to your geographic region in the U.S. Alcohol such as scotch, vodka, gin, and imported wines make good group gifts. Engraved quality items make good gifts, whether to groups or to an individual.

When invited to somebody's home, appropriate gifts include wine, chocolates, flowers, nuts, or fruits.

If you know your host has children, it would be a nice gesture to bring them small games or candy; U.S.-made candy and games will be especially well received. Make sure the products you present as gifts are not easily accessible in Colombia.

Avoid giving things that may be considered too personal, such as jewelry, clothing, ties, and body lotion.

### Greetings and Introductions

Greetings are very important to Colombians. In fact, the Colombian greeting is more extensive and involved than that of any other Latin American country. First and foremost, avoid greeting a group as a whole; rather, greet each person individually with a handshake. Doing this conveys respect and sincerity.

North Americans often greet with a brief handshake and a few general questions. In Colombia, greetings are a more extensive process. Make an attempt to engage each person fully, asking questions to demonstrate your interest in him or her. It is best to let your counterpart take the lead and go with the flow. Don't hurry to complete the greeting and advance to the next level; if you do, your entire venture may be in vain.

As business relationships turn into personal friendships, men may greet each other with a hug or a pat on the back. In the same way, women may greet other women by taking hold of each other's forearms.

An individual in Colombia can be addressed by using the titles Mr. (*Señor*), Mrs. (*Señora*), or Miss (*Señorita*), followed by the person's surname.

Recognition and status are very important to Colombians. In most cases, a high-ranking person or individual with a university degree is addressed as Doctor. If the person happens to be a woman, she is addressed as Doctora.

You should be aware that the majority of Latin Americans carry both their mother's and father's surnames. The father's surname is listed first and is used to address the individual. For example, *José Marquez García* would be addressed as *Señor Marquez*. Note that when a women marries, she typically takes her husband's surname.

Finally, and very importantly, never use a person's first name until he or she has given you permission to do so.

## Hierarchy Is Important

Hierarchy plays an important role within Colombia's corporate structure. Although companies are specifically structured to leave the ultimate decision-making power in the hands of a few, businesses value individual priorities and the opinions and input of the group.

When doing business in Colombia, it is important to recognize the different levels of hierarchy, as well as their relationships on other levels. North Americans often recognize that decisions are made at the top, but fail to respect the value of lower-level employees. This is not so in Colombia, where it is recognized that failure to take the opinions of "lesser" employees into consideration could affect the outcome of major decisions, creating potentially fatal mistakes.

### How Decisions Are Made

Colombians value the input that others have to offer. Consequently, decisions are made by a few based on group consensus. However, this is a slow process, so you will have to exercise patience as decisions are being made.

Although it is important to provide your Colombian associates with an attractive deal and all the facts, especially the bottom line, these things won't constitute deciding factors. Colombians base their decisions on feelings more than fact. Even if all your facts line up well and there is clearly profit to be made, if your counterpart "just doesn't feel good about it," then you can kiss your business good-bye.

### Meeting Manners

Choosing your company's representatives could be the most important decision you make in dealing with Colombian businesses. Colombians feel they are meeting with a specific person, not just a "company mouthpiece." For this reason, it is crucial you find the right individuals to meet with your Colombian counterparts—and to do so consistently. Changing your representatives during negotiations means that you will be starting back at "square one," and that can count against you.

The second most important decision you may make in dealing with Colombians is your choice of a third-party intermediary. The fact of the matter is that if you want to do business in Colombia, you are going to need a contact. Due to the emphasis on personal relationships and sense of business community, it would be very difficult for an "outsider" to waltz in and begin talking business. A third-party member will bridge the crosscultural gap, enabling you to do business more effectively. The Colombian-American Chamber of Commerce, located in Bogotá, may be able to assist you in finding a local Colombian agent. Note that a Colombian contact may also assist you with flight reservations and hotel reservations, as well as transportation to each destination.

Give a significant amount of consideration to the Colombian agent you choose. Because Colombians want to do business with people, not just company representatives, changing your contact at any time could be a disastrous move.

In a meeting, always engage in small talk before discussing business. This will let your colleagues know that your relationship with them takes priority over business. If possible, allow your Colombian associates to initiate the business discussion. Never leave as soon as the meeting is over; this will insult your colleagues and communicate that you have somewhere more important to be. Instead, engage in some more small talk and pleasantries before considering the meeting concluded.

Be sure to schedule any meetings at least two to three weeks in advance. Do not arrange back-to-back meetings. Instead, give yourself two to three hours between each.

Business matters that North Americans often resolve by phone or fax are resolved through face-to-face meetings in Colombia. Thus, doing business with Colombians will probably entail a number of personal meetings.

Be sure to have all documents and meeting materials translated into Spanish before your trip to Colombia. Visual aids are also very valuable in making your point.

Although your high-ranking Colombian associates may speak English, it is still advisable to provide an interpreter. If you fear this may offend your counterparts, simply ask beforehand if an interpreter should be present at a meeting.

As a follow-up to your meeting, it is a good idea to send a brief thank-you note, as well as a written confirmation of things that were discussed and any conclusions that were reached.

Most importantly, be patient! If you understand beforehand that it will take a particularly long time to accomplish even trivial business matters in Colombia, then you are already ahead of the game.

## *Punctuality*

Your Colombian counterparts will expect you, as a foreigner, to be on time for all business meetings. However, although your Colombian counterparts will probably be punctual, you should still expect them to arrive 15 to 30 minutes late, excepting business meals or restaurant meetings. Because you may be kept waiting, be on the safe side and bring some reading material or work to do although you wait. Note that people of a higher rank are more likely to keep you waiting.

Lack of punctuality is probably the biggest stumbling block for North Americans doing business in Colombia. But don't assume that your Colombian counterparts are lazy or irresponsible due to their poor punctuality record—that could be a grave mistake!

If a Colombian businessperson says he or she will call the following day, or states that a project will be completed by the end of the day, don't be surprised if it takes a week or more. This is the norm in Colombia.

## *Seating Etiquette*

As in most Latin American countries, the host will sit at the head of the table and the hostess will be seated at the opposite end. The most senior female will be seated to the immediate right of the host, although the most senior male will be invited to sit to the immediate right of the hostess.

### Tipping Tips

When eating in restaurants, a gratuity is often included in the bill. If you were especially pleased with the service, leave a little something extra.

Porters should be tipped approximately $1 for each piece of luggage.

Taxi drivers typically receive a tip equivalent to 10 percent of the fare, but it usually depends on what part of the country you are visiting. Ask your Colombian colleagues whether or not taxi drivers receive a tip in any particular city.

### Toasting Etiquette

Although wine is usually served with meals rather than beforehand, it will be the beverage for toasting, especially when guests are present.

The appropriate way to toast is by lifting the goblet as you say "Salud!" or "To your health!"

### When You Are Invited to a Home

Colombians are a very hospitable and gracious people. It is a great treat to be invited to someone's home. Once you have received such an invitation, it is good etiquette to send flowers in advance or present a gift when you arrive. Roses do not have the same romantic connotations that they do in North America; therefore, they will be well received if sent ahead of time.

In most cases, it is appropriate to dress in a formal manner when visiting someone's home (skirts or dresses for women and suits for men). The only exception may be in coastal cities or regions that are extremely warm. If that happens, simply note what those around you are wearing and dress accordingly.

You can expect to be offered a variety of alcoholic beverages when invited to an individual's home. Be careful though, and remain conservative in your drinking!

Note that it is not uncommon for light snacks to be served prior to the meal.

Do not leave immediately following the meal; this would be perceived as rude. Instead, take some time to engage in conversation with dinner guests.

## Whatever You Do...

- Don't complain about the city you are visiting, cross-cultural differences, or something your counterpart has done to upset you. Complaining, especially from a foreigner, is frowned upon in Colombia.

- Don't assume you can accomplish your business in Colombia at a fast pace.

- Don't ever smoke without first asking permission from those around you.

- Don't assume a yes means yes and no means no in Colombia. Colombians are more likely to tell you what they think you want to hear in order to avoid confrontation.

- Don't simply ask your counterparts if a project (or whatever else you are expecting) has been completed or finished. When Colombians agree that something is complete, this often means it's more or less complete. Instead, ask if the project is ready to be sent, presented, printed, etc.

- Don't neglect to take safety precautions when in Colombia. Ask your counterparts what areas of the city could be considered dangerous. Both the murder rate and frequency of kidnapping is significantly higher in Colombia than in the United States.

- Don't expect Colombian coffee to be strong. On average, Colombian coffee is quite mild.

# Chapter 6

# Costa Rica

**9 reasons people do business in Costa Rica**

1. Foreigners may possess full ownership of both business and real estate in Costa Rica without being citizens.

2. Costa Rica has a stable, peaceful democratic government and no military forces.

3. Costa Rica is a country that believes in equal treatment of all races and social classes and actively embraces peaceful coexistence.

4. The country's privately owned national preserves and beauty brings great appeal to outsiders, especially those who applaud the country's conservation efforts.

5. Costa Rica is a regular exporter of products to the United States, including textiles.

6. The Costa Rican economy is agriculturally based, its top industries being coffee, bananas, and sugar production.

7. Tourism is also a major industry.

8. Costa Rica is a major importer of U.S.-made cars and other vehicles.

9. Costa Ricans value education and are proud to boast that "We have more teachers than soldiers."

Despite being in a region generally known for its turbulence, the Republic of Costa Rica provides calm stability for visitors and businesspeople alike, and is one of the world's most popular vacation spots. This is due primarily to its peaceful, friendly people, acres of forests and national parks, and key location on the Central American isthmus, with miles of beaches and preserves that protect the immense amount of wildlife, tropical forests, and bio-diverse flora and fauna.

Costa Rica, whose natives are often called *ticos*, shares borders with Nicaragua on the north and with Panama on the east. Surrounded by oceans, its beautiful Caribbean coast is more than 130 miles long, although its rocky, irregular Pacific coast is even longer, approximately 630 miles. The country itself is bisected by volcanic mountain chains that stem from the southeast to the northwest. Within the central portion is the Central Valley, or Meseta Central. Here is where more than half of Costa Rica's population of more than 3.5 million *ticos* live. Here, too, is where the capital city of San José can be found.

Very little is known about Costa Rica's earliest history due to the loss of indigenous tribes and the destruction of ancient ruins after Spanish settlers took control of the land. It was named by Christopher Columbus, who was so impressed by the country after his two-week stay in 1502 that he dubbed it "the rich coast." It became an independent nation in 1821, by which time coffee had become its primary export and coffee growers ran the government. In 1856, Costa Rica suffered an invasion by U.S.-born William Walker and an army of Nicaraguan slaves. Then-president Juan Rafael Mora quickly amassed a civilian army that repelled the invaders and unified the country. This event was soon followed by free elections.

Costa Rica has maintained a democracy ever because, with only rare attempts from rabble rousers to disrupt the status quo. In 1949, Costa Rica achieved true political distinction by not only giving women and blacks the right to vote, but also by disbanding its army. In this way, the country started to set precedents for peace initiatives that culminated in President Oscar Arias' receipt of the Nobel Peace Prize in 1987. More recently, the Social Christian Unity Party has risen to power and has targeted Costa Rica's economy in an effort to pull it out of a long recession. The country has long depended on its agricultural production; only within this century has it begun to focus on other industries and on creating more of a cultural identity.

# Statistics and Information

### *Air Travel*

When traveling by air to Costa Rica, you will probably fly into Juan Santamaría, which is approximately seven kilometers from San Jose. The most practical way to get into the city is by taxi.

### *Country Codes*

Costa Rica's country code is 506.

Costa Rican cities do not have city codes. However, in order to place a call to this country, a seven-digit number must be dialed first.

### Currency

Costa Rica's currency is called the *colon* (also spelled *colone*). One *colon* is equivalent to 100 *centimes*. Costa Rican bills come in denominations of 1,000, 500, 100, 50, 20 , 10 and 5 *colonies*. Coins are available in 50 and 25 *centimes*.

### Dates

Costa Ricans write their dates in the European standard format of day, month, and year. For example, January 30, 1999 would be written 30/1/99.

### Ethnic Makeup

Costa Rica's population is one of the most homogenous in Latin America, with approximately 96 percent of the people being of Spanish descent, with the remainder composed of mestizo, African, Indian, or Chinese ancestry.

### Holidays and Religious Celebrations

| | |
|---|---|
| January 1 | New Year's Day |
| January 11 | Juan Santamaria |
| March 19 | Feast of Saint Joseph |
| Mar/Apr | Good Friday and Easter Sunday |
| May 1 | Labor Day |
| June 29 | Saints' Day: Peter and Paul |
| July 25 | Annexation of the Guanacaste Province |
| August 2 | Our Lady of the Angels |
| August 15 | Feast of the Assumption |
| September 15 | Independence Day |
| October 12 | Columbus Day |
| December 8 | Immaculate Conception |
| December 25 | Christmas |

Attempt to schedule any meetings around these holiday dates. Be aware that holidays falling on Saturday or Sunday may lead to the closing of business at the beginning or end of the week. Also note that many Costa Ricans vacation during the months of April, December, and January. Be sure to check the region you visiting for local holidays and religious practices.

## Language

The official language of Costa Rica is Spanish, though English is understood by many upper-level executives and government officials (as well as educated citizens), especially in areas with a high tourist influx. Numerous dialects of both Spanish and English are also used.

## Religion

Roman Catholicism is Costa Rica's official religion. Protestantism, however, is growing in popularity among certain segments of Costa Ricans, and most blacks tend to be Protestant.

## Time Zone Differences

Costa Rica is:

- Six hours behind Greenwich Mean Time.
- One hour behind U.S. Eastern Standard Time.

## Weather

Costa Rica essentially has two seasons. One is described as the "green (or wet) season," a period when it rains during the months of May to November. The "dry season" lasts from December through April. The average temperature is 75°.

# Etiquette

### Business Attire

Keep Costa Rica's tropical climate in mind as you consider what to pack for your trip. Wear clothes made of light material to compensate for the heat. It is also advisable to pack plenty of extra items as a means of ensuring fresh attire on a regular basis. (Due to the extreme heat, Costa Ricans may change clothing a number of times throughout the day.)

For business purposes, men should wear dark conservative suits and quality dress shoes. Women should wear dresses, skirts, and blouses, as well as high heels, which are the norm for women in this country. Conservative dress should be your guide, especially for women, who should wear nothing that could be considered flashy or revealing.

Casual dress may be acceptable, depending on the city you are visiting. However, if you're uncertain about what may be acceptable, it is better to err on the side of formality.

### Business Card Etiquette

Be sure to have plenty of business cards when visiting Costa Rica, and have a Spanish translation printed on the reverse side. Present your card Spanish side up, so that your cross-cultural associate can read the card as it is being received.

### Business Entertaining/Dining

Breakfast is typically eaten between 6 p.m. and 7:30 a.m.; lunch is eaten between 11 a.m. and 1 p.m.; dinner is served between 7 p.m. and 8:30 p.m. Evenings are typically the most popular time to entertain in Costa Rica.

Never be late for a business meal. You can usually expect your Costa Rican counterpart to be punctual for lunch appointments or more formal entertaining at restaurants. What to wear when entertaining may vary, depending on the city you're visiting as well as the type of restaurant.

It is common for people to say *buen provecho* ("eat well") before they begin their meal.

*Table Manners:* Remember to always work from the outside in when deciding which utensils to use first. For example, the outermost fork would be used for eating appetizers. If the table setting contains a spoon located above your plate, use this to stir your coffee.

Be sure to offer food and beverages to others before serving yourself. Try not to refuse any food that you are offered the first time. If you don't care for it, at least take a few bites to be polite.

Don't chew with your mouth open or talk with a mouthful of food.

Do not be a glutton. Be sure to leave food on your plate to indicate that you are satisfied.

## Conversation

Good topics of conversation include sites to see in the city you're visiting, polite questions about children and family, Costa Rica's nature preserves, the beautiful landscapes and climate, politics, and sports. Note that politics are an especially appropriate topic of conversation. Costa Ricans are very proud of their democratic government and their many years of peace.

Avoid asking personal questions about an individual's profession or family life. In addition, never say anything negative concerning Costa Rica.

Be sure to use good eye contact when conversing. It would be an insult to look away or not hold a steady gaze when talking to a Costa Rican.

Don't ever insult an individual, use sarcasm, or voice a complaint. Costa Ricans place great emphasis on personal respect.

Causing your counterpart to lose face will quickly end your business in Costa Rica.

### Gestures and Public Manners

Do not clench your fist with your thumb protruding between your index and middle fingers, as Costa Ricans consider this a vulgar gesture. (To clarify, this is the same gesture that is made when North American children play the game "I got your nose.") Otherwise you are generally safe to use familiar gestures, as Costa Ricans understand the majority of nonverbal cues that North Americans make.

Always cover your mouth when yawning, sneezing, coughing, etc.

Never place your feet on an office chair, a coffee table, or any type of furniture. This is considered a very unrefined act.

Avoid telling jokes or using sarcasm when doing business in Costa Rica; such humor may be easily misinterpreted.

Don't chew gum in public, even if you see others doing it.

Always offer a cigarette to other members of your party before having one yourself.

### Gift-Giving Etiquette

Business gifts are not normally exchanged in Costa Rica. One of the few exceptions to this rule occurs at Christmastime, but even then it is only between close friends.

When visiting someone's home, present the host or hostess with a small gift. Wine, flowers, candy, chocolates, and fruits make good gifts in this case.

Be careful not to present an individual with calla lilies; typically these flowers are associated with death and mourning.

### Greetings and Introductions

Be sure to shake hands with everyone you meet, and give each an individual acknowledgment with a smile and good eye contact. Note that Costa Ricans often give two-handed handshakes. As you become better acquainted with your Costa Rican counterparts, the level of affection will grow but not to the extent it does in other Latin American countries. The people of Costa Rica tend to be more reserved and businesslike. Nevertheless, it is very important to mirror your Costa Rican counterparts' enthusiasm when meeting and greeting. If you don't, offense may be taken.

An individual can be addressed by using the titles Mr. (*Señor*), Mrs. (*Señora*), or Miss (*Señorita*) followed by the person's surname.

Professional titles are very important to Costa Ricans, as they represent a symbol of status and accomplishment. It is therefore appropriate to refer to someone using his or her title followed by their last name. Examples: Doctor Ruiz, Lawyer Ruiz, President Ruiz.

Be aware that the majority of Hispanics use both their mother's and their father's surname. The father's surname is listed first and would be used to address the individual. For instance,: Carlos López Ruiz would be addressed as *Señor* López.

When a woman is married, she typically takes her husband's surname. However, some women keep their fathers' surnames for professional purposes.

### Hierarchy Is Important

Just as U.S. companies possess internal organizational structures, there is a definite pecking order in equivalent Costa Rican companies. For that reason, it is important to recognize that the top person will make the final decision after his team has shared their recommendations.

## How Decisions Are Made

Although high-ranking individuals are ultimately responsible for making decisions, group consensus typically dictates the outcome. Be sure to show respect for individuals at all levels of the company. Costa Ricans appreciate both equality and individuality; therefore, the opinions and perspectives of each person are valued.

The depth of your relationship with decision makers will strongly influence the outcome of negotiations. Be sure to work on developing personal friendships with your Costa Rican contacts.

Note that negotiations often move at a faster pace in Costa Rica compared to other Latin American countries.

## Meeting Manners

Be sure to arrive on time for meetings, or even a few minutes early. Your Costa Rican associates may surprise you by being as punctual.

Always schedule your meetings at least two or three weeks in advance. Once you have made the appointment, it is good to get a confirmation by phone or fax. You also should call and confirm the meeting again once you've arrived in Costa Rica. Note that initial meetings are often held in your Costa Rican associates' office.

To prepare for your meetings, have all written documents translated into Spanish before you arrive. Using colorful visual aids will make your presentations more enticing, although keeping the attention of your Costa Rican counterparts.

Always begin the meeting with small talk of some sort. Expect your Costa Rican colleagues to treat you with warmth and respect. Take your time making the transition into business, which should be initiated by your counterpart.

It is common for Costa Rican middle managers to be part of the first few meetings you attend. Upper-level managers typically take part in subsequent meetings, primarily because that is when the "meat and potatoes" negotiations will be taking place and when they may be able to add the leverage necessary to the talks. Because this is the case, it would be wise to follow the same strategy by inviting your own higher-level executive(s) to be part of a third or fourth meeting.

Be prepared and be patient. It is common for new issues to arise or disagreements to occur just as it seems things are coming to a close.

### Punctuality

As a foreigner, punctuality will be expected of you. Be prompt or perhaps a few minutes early for business meetings.

Costa Ricans are typically punctual for business meetings. Don't become irritated, however, if they arrive 15 minutes late.

### Seating Etiquette

Typically the person hosting the meeting will sit at the head of the table. You will be asked to sit to the host's right. When you are unsure where your Costa Rican contact would like you to sit, wait to be invited to sit down in the chair that is offered to you.

### Tipping Tips

Restaurants typically include the waitperson's gratuity in the bill, generally 10 percent. If you found the service especially pleasing, leave an extra 5 percent tip.

Porters should be tipped about 75 cents U.S. for each piece of luggage.

Typically, it is not necessary to tip taxi drivers. Ask your hotel concierge for the approximate taxi fare based on the distance you need to travel.

## Toasting Etiquette

Offering a toast in the Spanish (even if you haven't mastered the language) will be greatly appreciated by your Costa Rican counterparts. This is a wonderful way to bridge any cultural gaps. Latin Americans often say "Salud!" when offering a toast. If your counterparts offer a toast in your honor, it is a nice gesture to offer one in return later during the meal. Avoid making any attempts at humor although toasting; it could easily be misunderstood.

## When You are Invited to a Home

It is a great honor to be invited to a Costa Rican's home. Never reject such an invitation; your counterpart would be extremely offended.

When invited to a home, it is a nice gesture to present the host or hostess with a gift (see "Gift-Giving Etiquette").

Even if you don't care for coffee, be sure to accept it when offered to you. Not doing so may offend your host.

## Women in Business

Although Costa Rica has a reputation for encouraging equal treatment for all, the fact is that machismo is still very much the order of the day. *Tico* men love to flirt with women and expect a deferential attitude in return. Although the native *ticas* are making some headway against this attitude and other rampant discrimination, you are still unlikely to find too many women in management roles.

## Whatever You Do...

- Don't assume that a written contract will ensure long-term business in Costa Rica. If you want to maintain good business relationships, it is necessary to nurture the personal relationships that have developed during the course of your negotiations.

- Don't assume your hotel reservations are set until you have received a faxed confirmation.

- Don't ever refer to Costa Ricans as *"Ricans;"* this is considered very rude. Instead, bear in mind that the people of Costa Rica often refer to themselves as *"Ticos."*

- Don't assume a gift is special simply because it was made in the United States. Products from the U.S. are easily obtainable in Costa Rica.

- Don't assume that you will receive an embrace once you have established rapport with your Costa Rican contact. The greeting may continue to be a handshake, just as you would receive in the U.S.

- Don't invite your Costa Rican contact to lunch. Most people go home to enjoy this meal with their families. Plan on dinner instead.

- Don't linger after dinner when you are invited to another person's home. Just as in the U.S., Costa Ricans are early risers.

# Chapter 7

# Ecuador

## 7 reasons people do business in Ecuador

1. Television is an important source of advertising in Ecuador.

2. Ecuador is South America's largest oil producer; the country is rich in oil reserves.

3. Globally, Ecuador is a major exporter of coffee and bananas.

4. Ecuador is a democratic country that mandates voting privileges for all its citizens.

5. The government of Ecuador encourages international trade and welcomes foreign investors.

6. Agriculture is a major industry in Ecuador, employing at least 35 percent of the workforce.

7. Ecuador maintains a strong trading relationship with the United States and with other Latin American countries.

The name says it all: If this is the Republic of Ecuador, then we must be on the equator. Tucked into the northwestern corner of the South American continent, Ecuador—which is approximately the size of the U.S. state of Nevada—shares borders with Colombia on the north and Peru on the south and east; the Pacific Ocean lies along its western coast.

On its mainland, Ecuador has three distinct geographical regions: Costa (coastal lowlands in the western section of the country), Sierra (a.k.a. the Central Highlands), and Oriente (jungles in the Amazon basin, the easternmost portion of the country). The country also maintains control of the Galapagos Islands, located approximately 620 miles west in the Pacific Ocean, and home to an unusual array of plants and wildlife. The capital, Quito, is found in the northern region of the country, close to the equator, although its other best-known (and larger) city, Guayaquil, lies in the Central Highlands, on the banks of the Guayas River near the coast.

Ecuador's population is 11.7 million and growing. The majority of its people live in the Central Highlands, a region formed by two volcanic mountain ranges surrounding a main valley. Its government is a democratic republic, with an elected (one term only) president and a unicameral legislature.

As in other South American countries, details of Ecuador's ancient history, dating back to the Incas, have been lost over the years, although some ruins remain. Like many of its neighbors, Ecuador was conquered by the Spanish in the 1500s—a time when the Incans were effectively wiped out—and achieved independence in 1822 thanks to Simón Bolívar. Because that time, internal strife centering around the differences between the conservatives of Quito and the liberals of Guayaquil has frequently threatened the country's stability, and there have been numerous periods of military rule. In 1941, Peru invaded Ecuador and laid claim to much of its Amazonian region, an area that remains in dispute to this day, although both countries have attempted to suppress their squabbling in recent years in the interests of bolstering their respective economies.

Ecuador is a very Catholic country, and many of its holidays and celebrations are given over to religious feasting and festivals. Especially notable is Carnival season, just prior to Easter. At such times, tourists can enjoy the marvelous Andean music and crafts that distinguish the Ecuadorian culture.

# Statistics and Information

### Air Travel

Ecuador has two international airports: the Mariscal Sucre, and the Simón Bolívar. Taxis are available at both airports to take you to your destinations.

### Country Codes

The country code for Ecuador is 593.

City codes:

- 2 for Quito.
- 3 for Ambato.
- 7 for Cuenca.

## Currency

Ecuador's currency is called the *sucre*. One *sucre* is equivalent to 100 centavos. A s*ucre* is available in paper denominations of 1,000, 500, 100, 50, 20, 10, and 5. Coins come as 50, 20, and 10 centavos.

For changing money or cashing travelers' checks, rates are just as good at either banks or *casas de cambio* (exchange bureaus). Major credit cards also are accepted widely, and may even be used at automated teller machines—but watch out for the extra fees that may be assessed in these cases.

## Dates

Dates are written according to the European-style format, with the day followed by the month, then the year. For instance, July 15, 2005 should be written as 15/7/05. When writing the date in a sentence, inscribe it as "el 15 de julio" ("the 15th of July").

## Ethnic Makeup

Indians and mestizos together (in even proportions) account for approximately 80 percent of Ecuador's population, although 15 percent are of Spanish descent and 5 percent are African.

## Holidays and Religious Celebrations

| | |
|---|---|
| January 1 | New Year's Day |
| January 6 | The Epiphany |
| May 1 | Labor Day |
| May 24 | Commemoration of the Battle of Pichincha |
| July 24 | Bolivar's Birthday |
| August 10 | Independence Day |
| October 12 | Columbus Day |
| November 1 | All Saints Day |
| December 25 | Christmas Day |

## Language

The majority of Ecuadorians speak Spanish. Ecuadorians of Indian descent speak Quechua. Although English may be the language of business, be sure to check in advance to see if your Ecuadorian contact speaks English. Otherwise, make the necessary arrangements to have an interpreter.

Note that although English is understood throughout the business arena, very few individuals are fluent.

## Religion

The majority of Ecuadorians (90 percent) follow Roman Catholicism. Additionally, there are numerous, small Christian denominations throughout the country.

## Time Zone Differences

Ecuador is:

- Five hours behind Greenwich Mean Time.
- The same as U.S. Eastern Standard Time.

## Weather

Although there are generally two seasons, you will find that the climate of Ecuador will be different based on the part of the country you are visiting.

Be sure to take an umbrella in case you are there during the rainy season, which lasts from the end of the year through the first six months of each year.

Some areas are known for their unpredictability, with several climate changes sometimes occurring in a single day. Note that the Central Valley region maintains temperate, spring-like weather throughout the year.

# Etiquette

### Business Attire

In the Ecuadorian capital of Quito, professional attire will be expected in all business situations. This includes black or navy suits with white shirts for men and skirted suits and heels for women.

In some parts of Ecuador, it will be incredibly hot and humid. In these cases, be sure to wear natural fabrics that will allow your skin to breathe. However, you should keep casual business attire at home.

### Business Card Etiquette

Before going to Ecuador, be sure to have your business cards translated into Spanish on the reverse side. Your Ecuadorian contacts will appreciate the effort you've made, which tells them you want to conduct business based on their comfort level.

Titles are important to Ecuadorians. If you have a professional title, be sure to list it on your card as this will make a good impression, whether you are a *doctor* (medical or Ph.D.), *professor*, or *ingeniero* (engineer).

Note that government-affiliated employees may not have business cards; this is something to keep in mind to avoid embarrassing situations when meeting with these individuals.

### Business Entertaining/Dining

Lunch is the main meal of the day and is usually taken between 1 p.m. and 2 p.m. If you are invited to dinner, prepare to eat as late as 11 p.m. Following dinner, you will be expected to stay for a few hours to enjoy the *sobremesa,* or after-dinner conversation.

You will find that the majority of Ecuadorian men may feel obliged to pick up the bill when eating in a restaurant with a woman. For that reason, women who initiate a luncheon invitation should discreetly make arrangements to take care of the bill away from the table.

Just as Ecuadorians take note of what you wear, they will be equally impressed when you invite them to a restaurant that is known for its cuisine. One way to find out which restaurants are considered outstanding is to check with your hotel staff.

### Conversation

Your Ecuadorian contact will be proud of the history and culture of his/her country. Thus, you will find it helpful to bone up on this information to demonstrate your interest.

Just as in many other Latin American countries, families make for a good topic of conversation. Topics to avoid include sharing any views you may have about the superiority of the U.S. standard of living. You should also stay away from political topics; if something about Ecuadorian politics is brought up, listen to the discussion without expressing your opinion.

Finally, be sure not to bring up Peru as a topic of conversation; Ecuador and this country have had their problems, and the subject is a sensitive one to their citizens.

### Gestures and Public Manners

Like other Latin Americans, Ecuadorians are very comfortable when in close proximity to others. For that reason, don't back away when your contact is closer than you would like him or her to be. Also be aware that Ecuadorians are a very animated "touchy feely" people. If you are patted on the back or touched on the arm, recognize that it is very much part of the Ecuadorian communication style.

### Gift-Giving Etiquette

When you go to Ecuador, be sure to have gifts in hand. Items that will be appreciated include anything electronic such as compact discs or audiocassettes, or a quality North American pen set.

If your Ecuadorian contact enjoys sports, an appropriate gift would be a jacket or cap with your local team's name on it.

You may find it important to take along gifts that have been made specifically for women, such as scarves, perfume, and other personal items produced in the U.S.

If you choose to give flowers, avoid marigolds, because they are associated with funerals.

## *Greetings and Introductions*

When first meeting your Ecuadorian contact, the appropriate greeting is a handshake. Once your contacts are comfortable with you, you may receive an embrace or a kiss on both cheeks. Ecuadorian men typically embrace, although women give each other air kisses.

Above all, be sure to maintain good eye contact although meeting and greeting your Ecuadorian counterparts. As in other Latin American countries, eye contact is very important.

Make sure you know the correct pronunciation of names. It will be taken as an insult if you mispronounce an individual's name, so practice beforehand if you are unsure.

Avoid rushing greetings with your crosscultural associates; instead, take the time to show a sincere interest in them on an individual basis. Engage in small talk, smile, and allow your host to lead the flow of conversation. Be sure to shake hands and greet everyone in your party. If possible, try to avoid group greetings.

## *Hierarchy Is Important*

There is a definite pecking order in Ecuadorian business structures. Although middle managers may attend meetings with you, the high-level managers will ultimately be responsible for making decisions.

### How Decisions are Made

Technically, decisions are made by group consensus. However, the most senior executives have the last word. If you want to get anything accomplished, your best bet is to go to the top.

Be prepared. The negotiating process in Ecuador is often strenuous and drawn out and will require patience on your part.

Note that many Ecuadorian companies must receive approval from their purchasing committees. Be patient although this process is taking place. It may be in your best interest to schedule meetings with purchasing-committee members.

### Meeting Manners

If possible, avoid jumping right into business at the start of a meeting. Instead, engage in pleasantries to create a comfort level with your Ecuadorian contacts. Meetings in this country typically reflect a relaxed tone rather than one that is very rigid.

Your business contacts in Ecuador may not speak English. For that reason, prepare to have an interpreter be a part of your meetings.

Be aware that Ecuadorians "drive a hard bargain." They believe a price can always be lowered, so prepare yourself for tough negotiating.

### Punctuality

Ecuadorians have a double standard when it comes to punctuality. On the one hand, you will be expected to be prompt. On the other hand, you may have to wait for as long as 30 minutes for your Ecuadorian contact to arrive.

The exception to this is any invitation you may receive to a social gathering, in which case it is best to arrive approximately 30 minutes after the appointed hour. If you arrive on time, your host may not be ready to receive you.

### Seating Etiquette

Seating etiquette in Ecuador differs from many other Latin American countries. Here, the head of the table typically is offered to the guests of honor, with the host and hostess seated next to them.

### Tipping Tips

When you are in a restaurant, be sure to add a 15 percent tip on top of the bill's total.

It is not necessary to tip taxi drivers unless they have provided an added service such as assisting you with your luggage. When this is the case, give them a $1 tip. The same applies to hotel porters; be sure to acknowledge their assistance by giving them the equivalent of $1.

### Toasting Etiquette

The appropriate way to propose a toast is by lifting your goblet and saying "Salud!" as you look at the person being honored.

### When You Are Invited to a Home

It is a compliment to be invited to an Ecuadorian home, for it means that you have been accepted and your Ecuadorian contact would like you to become better acquainted with him by meeting his family. Be sure to bring a gift with you, ideally a box of fine chocolates or other candy from the U.S. that may not be available in Ecuador.

In some cultures, it is best not to compliment what you see in a person's home as they might feel obliged to give it to you. However, this is not the case in an Ecuadorian home, and you should feel free to comment on your surroundings without fear of being misinterpreted. It also is appropriate to let your hostess know how much you have enjoyed her meal and the time spent with her family.

Rather than overextending your stay, make a point to leave around an hour after dinner is finished.

## *Women in Business*

Many Ecuadorian women work outside the home; in fact, many are in high-level management positions. For that reason, Ecuadorian men likely will accept working with businesswomen from overseas. However, women doing business in this country should make a point of maintaining a professional demeanor at all times.

## *Whatever You Do...*

- Don't drink hard liquor if you are a woman. Stick with a wine, fruit juice, or nonalcoholic beverage.

- Don't recommend to "Go Dutch" when the restaurant bill arrives. Ecuadorians do not believe this is an appropriate way of handling a bill.

- Don't forget that you may be affected by the requisite altitude.

- Don't take a photo. Many people believe that having a photo taken of them is personally intrusive, although others may regard a camera as a portent of an "evil eye."

# Chapter 8

# Guatemala

---

**9 reasons people do business in Guatemala**

1. In recent years, Guatemala has experienced strong economic growth.

2. The exportation of bananas and sugar constitute major industries in Guatemala.

3. Guatemala is increasing its export of manufactured products, giving it more of a competitive edge with its Latin American neighbors.

4. Guatemala's government has signed numerous international agreements and treaties that promotes national security and reassures foreign investors; it is committed to free market policies.

5. Guatemala's agrarian industry is very strong, allowing for a variety of agricultural products.

6. Guatemala is located just an hour and a half away from both Miami and Mexico City, making it easily accessible to tourists.

7. The country has strong communication and travel networks.

8. Guatemala's large labor force includes skilled artisans.

9. Guatemala enjoys low taxes, a low inflation rate, and a stable currency.

---

A lush, colorful, and historical country, the Republic of Guatemala lies in the westernmost portion of Central America. It shares borders with Mexico on the north, Belize on the northeast, and El Salvador and Honduras on the east. Although smaller in size than many other Latin American countries—encompassing just 42,500 square miles—it is nonetheless home to 11 million people and more than 30 active volcanoes (among the highest in the world). The landscape is varied; in addition to the volcanoes located in the western highlands, there are numerous jungles and stretches of rich, fertile soil in El Petén, the country's lowlands, as well as two coastlines: the black-sand beaches that run along the Pacific Ocean, and a small, beach-free coast on the Caribbean Sea.

Guatemala's extensive history is reflected not just in the traditions and culture of its indigenous Indian tribe, the Mayans, but also in the bones and artifacts found within its borders, especially the dinosaur bones found in El Petén. The Mayan civilization was almost in ruins by the time Pedro de Alvarado conquered Guatemala for Spain in 1523, but subsequent colonization and the imposition of Catholicism nearly destroyed the culture entirely. Though the Maya have survived, even today they often are discriminated against and abused by the democratic Guatemalan government.

Guatemala achieved independence from Spain in 1821, and there followed a succession of governments whose rule was often marred by internal disputes with political factions vying for control. When the country's Communist Party appeared to be getting stronger in the early 1950s, the U.S. Central Intelligence Agency helped to organize a military coup. This was followed by a period of civil war and increased military suppression of the poorer classes, who were getting poorer at the expense of the rich classes who were enjoying the economic booms of the 1960s and 70s. When the United States severed military assistance, free elections were finally held and it seemed that Guatemala was on its way at last to political stability. However, civil war continued and successive leaders only recently have been able to bring both some measure of peace and a reduction in the military's involvement in governmental affairs.

There is still a great disparity between Guatemala's wealthy and working classes, but the Mayan heritage is evident in the apparel, crafts, and habitats of a large portion of the population. Nevertheless, Guatemala is surprisingly modern, with a vast communications and transportation network, and an active, European-style nightlife in its major cities.

# Statistics and Information

### Air Travel

The port of entry for Guatemala is La Aurora International Airport in Guatemala City. It is located only a few miles south of the capital, which makes for easy transport into the city by taxi.

### Country Codes

Guatemala's country code is 502. There are no city codes.

### Currency

Guatemala's currency is the *quetzal*. One *quetzal* is equivalent to 100 centavos.

The best place to exchange currency is in Guatemala City. Banks will provide the latest exchange rates, but you may also find *casas de cambio* in major airports. Guatemalan currency cannot be exchanged back into North American dollars when you leave, so be careful not to exchange more money than you think you will need. Note that U.S. dollars are the only foreign currency that can be exchanged in Guatemala.

It is becoming increasingly possible to get money with major credit cards at automated teller machines.

## Dates

As in other Latin American countries, dates are written with the day preceding the month, followed by the year. Therefore, January 30, 1999 would be written 30/1/99. If you were writing this date in longhand, it should read "el 30 de *enero* de 1999."

## Ethnic Makeup

*Mestizos* make up 56 percent of the country's population, although Mayans account for 44 percent.

## Holidays

| | |
|---|---|
| January 1 | New Year's Day |
| Early Apr  (Wed-Sun) | Easter |
| May 1 | Labor Day |
| June 30 | Army Day |
| August 15 | Assumption Day |
| September 15 | Independence Day |
| October 20 | Revolution Day |
| November 1 | All Saints Day |
| December 24 | Christmas Eve |
| December 25 | Christmas Day |
| December 31 | New Year's Eve |

## Language

Guatemala's official language is Spanish. About 23 percent of the population speaks one of two dozen Indian languages. You will find that English is widely understood, especially among the business class.

## Religion

There is no official religion. Throughout history, Roman Catholicism has been the leading religion in Guatemala. However, because the 1950s, many Guatemalans have converted to Protestantism and some now follow a combination of Roman Catholic and Mayan beliefs.

## Time Zone Differences

Guatemala is:

- Six hours behind Greenwich Mean Time.
- In the same time zone as U.S. Central Time.

## Weather

The climate in Guatemala varies from region to region, and much depends on whether you go during the wet or dry season.

Along the Pacific coast, you are likely to encounter extremely hot, humid, tropical weather, although the highlands are warm and comfortable during the dry season (October to May) and quite chilly during the rainy season, when temperatures can drop down to freezing at night.

Your best bet is to check in advance the climatic conditions for the area of the country that you'll be visiting.

# Etiquette

### Business Attire

Guatemala's weather will dictate the type of fabrics you should wear. However, do not assume that the heat will allow you to wear shorts or low-cut, revealing clothing. For business purposes, men should wear suits and ties in light or dark colors, although women should wear professional skirts and blouses. Note that women should never wear pants for business or business entertaining.

*Important:* Military clothing is *illegal* in Guatemala. For your own safety, avoid wearing suits of military colors or style.

### Business Entertaining/Dining

Business meals are more commonly scheduled for breakfast or lunch than at dinner time. Before discussing business at dinner, gauge your host's attitude to determine whether he views the occasion as social.

It is appropriate to include your spouse at dinner functions, provided the spouses of your Guatemalan counterparts also will be present.

It is common to engage in drinking and light appetizers before the meal. Women should only have one beverage before dinner. Coffee usually follows all meals.

Meals are often served on platters from which you help yourself. However, in some homes there may be a maid who will serve each person individually.

When serving yourself, be sure to take only what you can eat. In Guatemala, it is considered rude to leave food on your plate.

Etiquette for paying a restaurant bill is not clearly defined in Guatemala. If one person indicates he would like to pick up the check, show your appreciation and allow him to do so. Otherwise, each person should pay individually.

If you are hosting a meal at a restaurant, do not assume that your bill will be brought to you when the meal is concluded; rather, you will need to ask your waiter to bring the check when you are ready. To attract the attention of your waiter, simply raise your hand in a discreet fashion.

## Conversation

Before you visit, read up on Guatemala's history, traditions, and culture. Your Guatemalan counterparts will be very impressed and flattered if you show interest in and knowledge about their country. Appropriate topics of conversation include travel, children, popular sports, and cultural activities.

Don't be surprised or offended if you are questioned about your marital status, your family, or other personal matters shortly after making a new acquaintance. These topics are considered "fair territory" in Guatemala.

You should avoid mentioning Guatemalan politics or the continuous violence that has plagued the country for many years.

Guatemala is a "macho" country. In mixed company, men will be the ones who speak up and dominate conversation as the women sit passively and listen.

## Gestures and Public Manners

When speaking with Guatemalans, be sure to keep a moderate, soft tone. Always use steady eye contact to maintain interest and not come across as rude.

Don't point when calling someone over to you. Instead, use your entire arm, palm facing the ground, and make a sweeping gesture toward your body.

Waving good-bye is done by raising your hand, with your palm facing you and waving your fingers at yourself.

Do not use either the American "thumbs up" or the "okay" sign; these are considered obscene gestures in Guatemala.

Do not take photographs of any religious ceremonies, personal property, or people without obtaining permission first.

### Gift-Giving Etiquette

Though it is acceptable and appreciated to exchange gifts with your Guatemalan business associates, it need not be done during the first meeting. Wait until subsequent visits have established a relationship, or the deal is finalized.

It is a nice gesture to inquire of your associates what special thing they would like to have from the United States. Gifts of special interest to Guatemalans include small electronic gadgets, popular novels and best sellers, and the traditional bottle of liquor or wine.

### Greetings and Introductions

It is important that greetings are taken seriously. An individual greeting and handshake should be given to everyone you meet, whether in a business meeting or a social function.

Beware the firm grip! In Guatemala, handshakes should be limp whether exchanged with males or females. Two women greeting may pat one another on the forearm or exchange kisses on the cheeks. Two men meeting may embrace one another or exchange pats on the back.

Titles denote respect and are very important to Guatemalans. Very often a title can stand alone, without a surname; examples of such titles include those for doctors, lawyers, architects, and professors. A general term, *Licenciado*, is used to denote a person who is a college graduate. This title should be used in combination with a surname.

### How Decisions are Made

Guatemalan businesspeople of different ranks often have the power to make decisions without deferring to a higher authority.

In fact, those individuals with decision-making power are often the people you meet with from the beginning.

### Meeting Manners

Personal relationships are essential to successful business transactions in Guatemala. Thus, do not rush into the details of a business deal in an effort to reach a quick conclusion. Allow time for friendly conversation and social encounters. Business dealings will take time and patience.

Never assume a hostile or insulting tone. You may find the slowness of business and decision making frustrating, but do not reflect that in your demeanor. Guatemalans have a strong sense of honor and any criticism may be taken as a personal attack.

### Punctuality

As in other Latin American countries, you should always be on time for business and social functions, even though you may be kept waiting by your Guatemalan counterparts.

### Seating Etiquette

In a social situation, the male guest of honor should sit in the chair to the left of the host, although the female guest of honor should sit to the host's right.

### Tipping Tips

The gratuity is not included in a restaurant bill. Therefore, be sure to tip the waiter about 10 to 15 percent, depending on how you liked the service.

Hotel porters should be given about $1 for each bag.

### When You Are Invited to a Home

Business should never be discussed when visiting a Guatemalan associate's home. Such invitations are considered purely social and a time to build personal relationships.

It is appropriate to bring a small gift for your host/hostess such as flowers (any color but white) or wine.

Do not feel obliged to rush out after a meal has reached its conclusion. Coffee will be served, and it is expected that you will stay and converse for a although. During the week, it is appropriate to excuse yourself around 11 p.m. On weekends, stay until midnight.

## Women in Business

Though there are many women in Guatemala's workforce, it is still a male-dominated society. It is very rare to see a woman in a position of management or power. Foreign businesswomen should conduct themselves in a professional, conservative manner.

## Whatever You Do...

- Don't present white flowers as a gift. They are reserved for funerals.

- Don't expect to complete your business deal during your first visit. The pace is slower in Guatemala and several trips may be required to close a deal.

- Don't forget that Guatemala businesses close in the afternoon for lunch and rest. Working hours are typically from 8 a.m. to noon, and from 2 p.m. to 6 p.m.

- Don't plan your business trip during the months of January, April, August, November, or December. These are popular vacation and holiday months.

- Remember to confirm all appointments two weeks in advance.

- Don't forget to have your business materials translated into Spanish before you leave for Guatemala.

# Chapter 9

# Mexico

## 8 reasons people do business in Mexico

1. Mexico borders the United States, has strong ties with Canada, and is a partner in the North American Free Trade Agreement.

2. The country also maintains close trade relationships with Germany, Japan, and the United Kingdom.

3. Mexico's government encourages foreign ownership of manufacturing facilities.

4. Mexico is rich in natural resources, including oil, ores, and minerals.

5. Among its major industries are the production of oil, petrochemicals, steel, automobiles and automobile parts, and fertilizer.

6. The export of coffee, seafood, and agricultural products comprise a major part of the Mexican economy.

7. Mexican businesspeople place a high emphasis on personal relationships when building professional relationships.

8. Haggling is an important part of the negotiating process in Mexico.

Mexico—formally called the United Mexican States—is the United States' closest Latin American neighbor, both geographically and economically. Located at the very north of the Central American isthmus, Mexico is bordered on the north by the U.S., and on the southeast by Guatemala and Belize. It is otherwise surrounded by water, with the Pacific Ocean lying to the west and south, the Gulf of California on the northwest (between Mexico and the Baja California peninsula), and the Caribbean Sea off the coast of the Yucatán Peninsula. There are numerous mountain ranges that mark Mexico's terrain, which is as varied as the country is vast. Beaches, lowlands, rainforests, deserts, and savannahs all form parts of the Mexican landscape. However, human and animal encroachment on the land and its resources have resulted in only about a fifth of the land remaining arable. Most of the population of 96 million are concentrated in urban areas, including the capital, Mexico City, where 20 million people live.

Mexico has an extensive history dating back to at least 20,000 years before the arrival of Christopher Columbus in the New World, and probably even earlier than that. Mayan and Aztec civilizations flourished in this land before Spanish invaders arrived and began to kill off most of the Indian population. The Spanish held dominion over the country until 1821, when a strong resistance movement managed to achieve independence. There followed many years of instability, with numerous changing governments and border disputes with the U.S. that resulted in significant losses of Mexican territory to its northern neighbor. After the U.S. annexed Texas in 1845, the Mexican-American War erupted. Subsequently, Mexico ceded not just Texas but large portions of other territories on the North American continent. When France later attempted to colonize the country, still more wars were fought as Mexico struggled to remain a free and independent nation.

From 1878 to 1911, Porfirio Diaz ruled Mexico with an iron fist, achieving economic and political stability but also the discontent of his citizens, who finally revolted against his dictatorship. The subsequent civil war, called the Mexican Revolution, lasted for 10 years and cost almost two million lives. Once this crisis had passed, the Party of the Institutionalized Revolution (PRI) took the reigns of the country, which it still maintains today despite occasional resistance to the one-party political system.

An oil boom in the 1970s led to a glut in the 1980s that caused a massive recession leading to increased murmurs of discontent. In 1988, Carlos Salinas de Gortari was elected president and immediately set about instituting economic reforms designed to combat inflation and bring the national debt under control. This in turn led to the establishment of the North American Free Trade Agreement in 1974, at the time a major triumph for Salinas and his supporters. Further protests brought about Salina's removal from office and the election of Ernesto Zedillo, whereupon the country slid even further into debt and to the point of bankruptcy. With help from the U.S. and other nations, Zedillo has managed to pull his country further and further away from the brink, instituting economic reforms and declaring his support for a fully democratic society and government.

Today, Mexico is growing in strength as a nation and is certainly a leader among its Latin American neighbors.

# Statistics and Information

### Air Travel

When flying into Mexico City, you will arrive at the Benito Juarez Airport. Taxis are a practical way of getting to the city. If you would like to share a ride, go to a ticket booth at the airport that says *colectivo* and make arrangements there. If you would prefer to go directly to your hotel rather than make several stops along the way, purchase a ticket for a taxi that is *especial*.

### Country Codes

Mexico's country code is 52.

City codes:

- 5 for Mexico City.
- 3 for Guadalajara in Jalisco.
- 322 for Puerto Vallarta.
- 353 for Mazamitla in Jalisco.

### Currency

The *peso* is the currency of Mexico. One peso equals 100 centavos. Pesos are available in denominations of 10,000, 5,000, 500, 100, & 50 bills.

The best places to exchange money are in banks and in *casas de cambio*. However, bear in mind that banks only transact currency exchanges during certain hours. Major credit cards are accepted just about anywhere in Mexico.

### Dates

Mexico practices the European standard format of listing the day of the week first followed by the month, then the year. For instance, February 15, 2002 is written as 15/2/02. When writing out the date in a letter, the appropriate way to do so would be "el 15 de *febrero* de 2001."

## Ethnic Makeup

The population of Mexico is composed of many ethnic backgrounds. The majority of Mexicans (approximately 80 percent) are mestizos, which is a combination of Spanish heritage and Meso-American Indian background. In many parts of Mexico, citizens' backgrounds reflect different civilizations. For instance, the people of Merida, which is in the Yucatan, have a strong Mayan influence. By contrast, Oaxaca, which is in the southern part of Mexico, is representative of the Zapotec and Mixtec civilization.

## Holidays and Religious Celebrations

| | |
|---|---|
| January 1 | New Year's Day |
| January 6 | The Epiphany |
| February 5 | Constitution Day |
| February 24 | Flag Day |
| March 21 | The Birthday of Benito Juarez |
| March 23 | Holy Week followed by Easter |
| May 1 | Labor Day |
| May 5 | Cinco de Mayo (Commemorates victory over the French at the Battle of Puebla) |
| September 1 | National Holiday |
| September 16 | Independence Day |
| October 12 | Columbus Day |
| November 20 | Revolution Day |
| December 25 | Christmas Day |

## Language

Spanish is the main language spoken in Mexico. There are more than 50 indigenous languages.

Although some people may have a working knowledge of English, anyone doing business with Mexicans will find that it is in their best interest to learn several key Spanish phrases in order to establish rapport. When learning such phrases, it is important to focus on addressing your Mexican contacts in the more formal manner-that is, using the *usted* form of speaking, particularly with individuals of higher rank and people much older than you-because this demonstrates respect. When your Mexican contact asks you to use the *tu* form, it means that person is comfortable communicating with you on a first-name basis, allowing you to adopt a more informal manner.

### Religion

More than 90 percent of Mexicans are Roman Catholics. In fact, this religion is very much intertwined into the Mexican heritage, as is evident by the country's many religious holidays. Approximately 6 percent of the country follow Protestant faiths, although the remainder practice the beliefs of various other Indian cultures.

### Time Zone Differences

Most of the country is:

- Six hours behind Greenwich Mean Time.
- Baja is on Pacific Time.
- East of Baja is on Mountain Time.
- Central Mexico, including Mexico City, Vera Cruz, and Chihuahua, are on Central Time.

### Weather

Mexico is said to have just two seasons: winter and summer. If you are in Mexico during the period of mid-May through October, which Mexicans consider to be winter, you will want to have an umbrella with you. Note that rain is most common during the middle of the afternoon and only lasts a short time.

The climatic conditions also will depend on which section of the country you happen to be in. Temperatures tend to be hot and humid along the coasts, but will be more temperate, and certainly more dry, in the higher inland regions. Note that the months of December to February tend to be cooler.

# Etiquette

## *Business Attire*

Mexicans dress with dignity no matter what the social class. They are also fastidious about their grooming and will expect the same of you. A clean and crisp appearance is an important factor to these people, whether one is dressed formally or informally. For business meetings, dark suits and ties are the norm; when the situation calls for you to dress in a business-casual mode, be certain that your shirts are clean and pressed, shoes are polished (a high gloss is common), and accessories project a sense of class.

Women doing business in Mexico should dress appropriately in skirted suits, hosiery, and heels. Although the "natural look" is common for many women in the U.S., this is not the case in Mexico. Make-up and ornate jewelry are an important part of dressing to Mexican women.

## *Business Card Etiquette*

Mexicans tend to have more business cards than their counterparts in other countries. Taxi drivers and bartenders may have a business card to share with you just as readily as any engineer, executive, or professor. For that reason, be sure to take more than the usual number of business cards with you.

Because your title or position is considered an important part of who you are, be sure to include it on your card, following your name. *Note:* Your Mexican contact will be especially impressed when you have your cards translated in Spanish on the reverse side.

## Business Entertaining/Dining

"Breaking bread" with your Mexican contact is vital to developing a long-term business relationship. However, bear in mind that these events are intended to be social in nature rather than a time for business to be discussed. Only bring up business if your host does so.

Although *el desayuno*, or breakfast, is a meal that is commonly taken at home with one's family, business breakfasts have become more common in Mexico in recent years. Note that Mexican breakfasts consist of hearty foods (for example, eggs and steak). You may also be invited to *el almuerzo* (lunch), typically around 2 p.m., or *la merienda* (dinner), usually around 9 p.m. or later. If your Mexican contact invites you out after work, this will most likely be a social occasion with appetizers and drinks.

Lunches are usually the main meal of the day and will last for a few hours. Dinners consist of lighter fare than what you may have enjoyed during the lunch hour. Fried tortillas and salsa are often served as appetizers.

Mexicans tend to use the continental style of dining, with the fork held in the left hand and the knife in the right. Soft tortillas are commonly used as a wrap for food, and thus are frequently lifted with the hands, just as a sandwich would be in the U.S.

When you are hosting a meal, bear in mind that many Mexicans may prefer to have a beverage served at room temperature, without ice. When paying for a meal at a restaurant, be sure to put the money or credit card directly into your *camarera's* (server's) hand. If you place it on the table, this could be interpreted as an indication that you do not want to have contact with the person.

## Conversation

Mexicans are very proud of their culture and heritage. For that reason, it is a good idea to familiarize yourself with Mexico and its history.

Topics of interest that you might pursue include your travel itinerary, what's going on in Mexico, *futbol* (soccer), sites you have visited in Mexico, the weather, and your immediate surroundings. Be prepared for some personal discussions; Mexicans tend to talk about their families and private lives more than many other Latin Americans.

Topics that you should avoid include the Mexican-American War, Mexican politics, or any comparison between Mexico and the U.S. that may appear to put the latter in a position of superiority.

### Gestures and Public Manners

Although maintaining eye contact is important in other countries, this is not the case in Mexico. When you are talking with a Mexican, you should be sure to break eye contact regularly, otherwise you will be perceived as gawking at that person.

You will notice that touching arms and patting backs are very common gestures in Mexico. Once you have established rapport with a Mexican, you may even receive an embrace.

Keeping your hands in your pockets is considered rude in many countries outside the U.S., and Mexico is no exception. Hands above board!

When you sneeze, you may hear a person say "Jesús" or "Salud!"

Just as in many other Latin American countries, the "OK" gesture formed with the thumb and index finger should be avoided, because it is considered vulgar.

Although Mexicans are proper in many ways, this does not apply when they are standing in *colas* (lines). Instead of waiting patiently, they tend to push their way to the front of the line. Be prepared for this to happen to you!

Form is an important part of the Mexican culture, so "packaging yourself" *con elegancia* in both your surroundings and your dress will go a long way in the eyes of your Mexican contacts. In this regard, where you stay in Mexico undoubtedly will be taken into account. For instance, if you stay in the *Zona Rosa*, you most likely will impress your Mexican colleagues.

### *Gift-Giving Etiquette*

Although gifts are exchanged at the beginning of business relationships in many societies, this is not the case when first establishing rapport with colleagues in the Mexican culture. However, once you get to know someone, taking a small gift to a meeting would be both appropriate and appreciated. It is also a good idea to have gifts in hand when first meeting your Mexican contact's family members and during subsequent gatherings.

Appropriate gifts include items made in the U.S. or a book about the city you represent.

### *Greetings and Introductions*

Shaking hands is the most common way of meeting and greeting in Mexico. Rather than offering a "bone-crusher" handshake, a light grip will do. Just as in the United States, the handshake should be used both at the beginning of a meeting, as a way of establishing rapport, and when leaving at the conclusion, as a way of solidifying what was discussed. Women should initiate all handshakes with men.

You will notice that Mexican males who have an established rapport may offer each other an *abrazo* (hug).

When meeting others, address them as *Señor, Señora* or *Señorita*, followed by their last names. If you do not know somebody's last name, it is appropriate to simply address him or her as *Señor, Señora* or *Señorita*.

Mexicans commonly have two surnames that are hyphenated, the first being their father's last name and the second their mother's last name. Unless you are asked to do otherwise, use both names when addressing somebody. Mexicans may shorten their names according to personal preference, and may choose either their father's or their mother's name. For example, Señor Gonzalez-Ruiz might encourage you to call him simply Señor Gonzalez. You might also see names written out with the last name reduced to an initial—for example, José Gonzalez R.

Individuals who have earned degrees and have titles such as "*Profesor*," "*Doctor*," "*Ingeniero*" (engineer), and the like should be addressed by these titles, followed by their last names. Once you have a good rapport established with these persons, you may drop their last names and refer to them using their professional titles. For instance, when greeting Profesor Ruíz, you would say, "Buenos días, Professor."

### Hierarchy Is Important

Mexican companies comprise top executives, managers, and workers. Although many individuals may be asked their opinions on decisions, the person who will have the last say will be the top person in authority.

### How Decisions are Made

What you know is important; however, who you know is even more so. If you have established a personal relationship with your Mexican contact, then you have laid a good foundation for your working relationship with that company. Note that although others may offer input, the person in authority usually will make the final decision.

Prepare for lengthy and involved negotiations with your Mexican contacts. Haggling is very much a part of the decision-making process. When an agreement is reached, you will receive a verbal confirmation; make sure that this is followed in turn by a written agreement.

### Meeting Manners

As you prepare for a trip to Mexico, it is important to confirm in advance any appointments you have made. Make a point of calling or faxing to confirm your meeting times and locations. When possible, your correspondence should be prepared in Spanish. If you are not fluent in the language, at the very least you should integrate terms such as *Buenos días* and *Gracias* into your correspondence.

Business relationships in Mexico are based on trust. One way that Mexicans develop trust is by taking some time to establish rapport before getting to the business at hand. When possible, one of your organization's highest-ranking managers should be part of the entourage traveling to Mexico to establish ties.

It is important to remain flexible during meetings. More often than not, there may not be a formal agenda; even when there is, a lot of deviation may take place. If you perceive that the topic that you expected to discuss is not going to be brought up, just go with the flow. By acting relaxed and not pushing, you will actually be accomplishing more in the long run.

Mexicans enjoy form as much as they do substance. Your presentation should be eloquent in style rather than "cut and dried." How your presentation materials look will affect on your Mexican contact's decision to do business with you.

Note that when you are asked to get together again in *ocho días*, this is one week from the day you are meeting, not eight days. In other words, if it is Monday and your Mexican contact says he would like to schedule another meeting *en ocho días,* he is indicating that he would like to get together the following Monday.

When you are in a meeting, be sure not to challenge or correct your Mexican contacts in any way. Instead, allow them to "save face" by discussing errors or misunderstandings privately, after the meeting. Correcting somebody in front of others will not only embarrass that person; others in the meeting will shun you as a direct result of it.

## *Punctuality*

When interacting with Mexicans, it is important to understand that their viewpoint on time is much different from the way *gringos* think about it. Most Mexicans feel that Americans allow the clock to control them rather than the other way around. For that reason, Mexicans differentiate time in two ways: *la hora americana,* or American time, and *la hora mexicana,* or Mexican time. *La hora americana* is best defined as "being on time." However, in *la hora mexicana,* one might arrive from 15 minutes to an hour after the agreed-upon time. When scheduling an appointment with a Mexican, be sure to ask if the scheduled time will be *en punto* (exact) or *más o menos*—that is, "more or less," meaning that you should prepare to wait when you arrive.

You should also recognize that the term *mañana,* which literally means both "tomorrow" and "morning," can have yet another connotation: "later." When you are told that something will be completed *mañana,* you should not expect it to be completed the next day, but rather at a point in time down the road. By understanding this, you will avoid setting unrealistic expectations for your Mexican contacts—or for yourself in waiting for something you think might be imminent.

## *Seating Etiquette*

Mexican seating etiquette dictates that the host sits at the head of the table, with his most senior guest to his immediate right. If you are the guest of honor, this is where you can expect to sit.

## *Tipping Tips*

Tipping is common in Mexico. In restaurants, 15 percent should be added to the bill. Porters should be given the equivalent of $1.00 for their assistance with a few pieces of luggage. Hotel chambermaids should also be left approximately $1 per day.

Taxi drivers should be tipped the equivalent of $1 more than the fare. When taking a taxi, be sure to take one that is marked. You should also be sure to ask what the fare will be before getting in the taxi. You will be able to get an approximate idea of what you should be charged either by asking the hotel concierge or by asking to look at the fare chart.

### Toasting Etiquette

When you are being toasted or are proposing a toast, the appropriate term to use is "Salud!"

### When You Are Invited to a Home

It is quite an honor to be invited to a Mexican's home. Be sure to arrive at least 15 minutes later than the time you are given; otherwise, the family may not be ready to receive you.

Be sure to go with gifts in hand for your host's spouse and children. An appropriate gift for the hostess includes a bouquet of flowers. Avoid giving yellow flowers (such as marigolds) because they are equated with mourning. Avoid red flowers as well, as this color may be misinterpreted to mean that you are putting a curse on the recipient.

Children will enjoy something from the U.S. such as toys, computer-related software, etc. If you are unsure, ask your Mexican contact the age of his or her children and what they enjoy doing. If they like sports, a baseball shirt or cap from your local team may be the perfect gift.

Be sure to express your appreciation for this invitation by acknowledging the hostess for the delicious meal, thanking your host, and sending a note of appreciation afterwards.

### Women In Business

Although women from abroad will be treated with a great deal of respect, they must earn it by maintaining a professional demeanor in their dress and actions. It is important for women to recognize that *machismo* is very strong in Mexico and that Mexican men are very proud. For that reason, if a businesswoman invites her Mexican contact to lunch, she should make arrangements to take care of the bill away from the table. Also, if a dinner invitation is extended, spouses also should be invited.

## *Whatever You Do ...*

- Don't wear shorts walking down the street. In Mexico, shorts are considered to be beachwear.

- Don't wear jeans or tennis shoes if you are on an official business trip. Rarely do Mexican businesspeople wear such casual attire.

- Don't forget your geography. Mexico is officially a part of North America. For that reason, be sure to recognize that Mexicans are also North Americans and may be offended if you give that designation only to citizens of the United States.

- Don't use the Lord's name in vain, as this will offend your Mexican contacts.

- Don't forget that Mexicans are very status conscious and likely to be impressed if they see you wearing designer clothes.

- Don't be surprised if your Mexican contact stands nearer than two arm's lengths to you. They are accustomed to close personal distances.

- Don't be surprised if your Mexican contact inquires about what certain things cost in the U.S. It is common for Mexicans to make comparisons of prices between countries.

# Chapter 10

# Panama

---

### 8 reasons people do business in Panama

1. The Panama Canal has been the key to trading in the western hemisphere because it was built.

2. Panamanians place a stronger importance on personal relationships than on material possessions.

3. The vast majority of Panama's population speaks English.

4. Panama is a country that places a high value on the importance of family.

5. Banking, shipping, agriculture, and tourism are among this country's strongest industries.

6. By air, Panama can be reached within two hours from Miami and three hours from New Orleans, making it very accessible to U.S. businesspeople.

7. Panama generally has been a peaceful country over the past century (with some exception).

8. The country is both culturally rich and technologically modern.

Geographically, Panama is an isthmus and the bridge that connects Central and South America; indeed, the shape of the country seems to convey that very impression, extending as it does from Costa Rica on the west to Colombia on the east. Its Caribbean coastline is 720 miles long, although the Pacific coast stretches for close to 1,050 miles. The width of the country varies, and at one point is only 30 miles wide. Panama also has numerous island groups off its coasts, many of which are great tourist attractions. Its best-known feature, however, is the Canal, an engineering marvel that essentially divides the country into eastern and western sections. Though Panama has two mountain chains running through it, it is primarily made-up of lowlands and rainforest, particularly in the northwestern area near the Canal Zone. This environment is home to a wonderful array of animal and plant life and has many nature preserves that protect its resplendent flora and fauna.

Panama's earliest Indian cultures, like so many in Latin America, were eliminated when the Spanish conquistadors arrived in the New World. From almost the start of its history, Panama frequently has been the center of discussions about ways to get from the Atlantic Ocean to the Pacific Ocean without traveling all the way around the southern tip of the continent. Eventually, the country became a province of Colombia, which initially exerted considerable control and signed a treaty with the United States in 1846, allowing the U.S. to build a railroad across the isthmus.

In 1880, France tried and failed to build a canal, and subsequently sold its rights to the United States. The U.S. then supported a rebellion that resulted in Panama's independence in 1903. Building of the canal that would link two oceans began in 1904 and was completed 10 years later. Today, it provides a significant passageway for over 12,000 vessels per year. However, it has proved to be a point of contention in Latin American affairs, particularly regarding U.S. interference in local policy, militarily and otherwise. The treaty was eventually renegotiated, and a new one signed in 1977 gives complete control of the Canal to Panama by 1999.

Meanwhile, by 1989 dictator (and drug trafficker) Manuel Noriega had taken forceful control of the country and in December of that year declared that Panama was at war with the United States. After an unarmed U.S. soldier was apparently killed, the U.S. quickly invaded the country for the presumed purpose of arresting Noriega and establishing a more peaceful democratic government. Although the invasion resulted in a considerable loss of civilian life, it also succeeded in putting Noriega behind bars; he is currently serving a 40-year sentence for money laundering.

Today, Panama has a democratically elected government that has been instituting many improvements, including economic and educational reforms.

# Statistics and Information

### Air Travel

Panama's Tocumen International Airport is a modern facility located one hour east of Panama City. Taking a taxi to the city will cost $12 U.S., but this fare can be split by riding with another passenger. Buses leave the airport for the city every 15 minutes and cost considerably less.

## Country Codes

Panama's country code is 507.

City codes:

- 44 for Colón.
- 77 for David.

## Currency

Panama does not have paper bills of its own, but rather uses U.S. currency. Bank notes are called *balboas*, with one balboa equal to $1. Coins in Panama are very similar to U.S. coins but have different engravings. Panamanian coins can be interchanged with American coins.

## Dates

As is common in Latin American countries, dates are written in the European standard format style, with the day preceding the month, which is followed by the year. Thus, January 30, 1999 would be written 30/1/99.

## Ethnic Makeup

Panama's population of only 2.5 million people is one of the smallest in Latin America. The majority (62 percent) are *mestizo*, although 14 percent are of African descent, 10 percent are Spanish, 5 percent are mulatto, and 5 percent are native Indians.

## Holidays and Religious Celebrations

| | |
|---|---|
| January 1 | New Year's Day |
| January 9 | Day of National Mourning |
| 4 days before Ash Wed. | Carnival |
| Mid-April | Good Friday-Easter |
| May 1 | Labor Day |
| August 15 | Panama City Day |

| | |
|---|---|
| November 1 | National Anthem Day |
| November 2 | All Souls Day |
| November 3 | Independence Day |
| November 4 | Flag Day |
| November 10 | First Call of Independence |
| November 28 | Independence from Spain |
| December 8 | Mother's Day |
| December 25 | Christmas Day |

## Language

Panama's official language is Spanish. However, most Panamanians, especially those in the business sector, are fluent in English. You may also hear some Indian languages spoken.

## Religion

There is no state religion in Panama, but more than 84 percent of its citizens are Roman Catholic. The remainder includes members of the Protestant, Muslim, and Hindu faiths.

## Time Zone Differences

Panama is:

- Five hours behind Greenwich Mean Time
- In the same time zone as U.S. Eastern Standard Time.

## Weather

There are only two seasons in Panama. The summer, which runs January through April, is dry and hot. The winter months, May through December, are rainy and humid. Climate and conditions will vary depending on your geographic location within Panama, so check beforehand to determine what you will need to pack for your trip.

# Etiquette

### Business Attire

Appropriate businesswear for men is finely tailored suits of dark colors. Women should dress conservatively in a tailored dress or skirt and blouse.

### Business Entertaining/Dining

Panamanians enjoy socializing, so the most successful business endeavors will result from the time spent developing personal relationships with your counterparts.

Always choose a fine restaurant when dining with business associates. To attract a waiter's attention, say *"Mozo"* or *"Señor."* Waitresses should be addressed as *"Señorita."* Drinks are often ordered before and during the meal. It is customary for the person who initiated the invitation to pay the bill.

In a private home, the family's maid often serves meals. She will serve each person individually or by placing large platters in the middle of the table, from which you can serve yourself. Attempt to eat everything on your plate. To indicate that you have finished eating, place your utensils vertically in the middle of your plate.

### Conversation

You will find Panamanians to be delightful conversationalists and because many speak fluent English, there should be little problem communicating. Sports are very popular in Panama. Soccer, basketball, boxing, and the national favorite, cockfighting, are always excellent topics. In addition, feel free to discuss family life, travel, and local culture.

Because there is some anti-American sentiment in Panama, be sure not to refer to things as being "Americanized." Avoid discussing politics and the former Canal Zone treaties.

### Gestures and Public Manners

The United States has had much influence in Panama. Gestures, both obscene and otherwise, are often in concert with American gestures.

Never take anyone's picture without obtaining permission first.

### Gift-Giving Etiquette

The exchange of gifts is not an essential part of a business relationship in Panama. However, after several meetings or upon completion of a contract, it is appropriate to present your counterparts with a modest token of appreciation. Gifts from your hometown, such as books, crafts, or small electronic devices are always appreciated.

If you will be visiting a private home, although it is not mandatory, a gift of wine, chocolate, or local crafts from the U.S. are a nice gesture.

### Greetings and Introductions

The etiquette for greetings and introductions is consistent with that practiced in the United States. Shake hands with everyone you meet. Once a relationship has been established, it is common for women to exchange kisses on the cheek and for men to kiss women on the cheek; two men will commonly only shake hands. At a social function, be sure to make the rounds and introduce yourself to everyone in attendance.

Titles are very important to Panamanians. Always address someone by their appropriate title, until you are invited to use a less formal address. *Liceniado* is a general title for anyone who has received a bachelor's degree and can be placed before a surname. Those with professional degrees, such as doctors, lawyer, architects, or professors, can simply be addressed by their title, without use of a surname. If a person possesses no professional or educational title, or you simply don't know what it might be, then utilize the Spanish forms of Mr., Mrs., and Ms: *Señor, Señora,* and *Señorita.*

## How Decisions are Made

You will find in Panama that great thought is placed into making important decisions. Although an individual rather than a committee will make decisions, this individual will place great emphasis on how the results of his decision will affect the entire group.

## Meeting Manners

Spend time getting to know your Panamanian associates personally before diving into business proceedings. Panamanians place great importance on personal relationships. If you have established a rapport outside the office, you will find your business transactions will be much smoother.

Always have any materials you plan to use translated into Spanish. This includes your business cards and brochures, charts, or literature you plan to distribute during your presentation.

Never attempt to flaunt your position or level of authority. Panamanians prefer to treat everyone equally. You rarely will see Panamanians publicly disagree or argue; therefore, you should avoid criticizing or reprimanding an associate in public. In addition, take care about what you hear; what you think is an affirmative response may simply mean your contact was being polite.

## Punctuality

In business, be on time for meetings and functions. However, the rules of punctuality are very different for social engagements. It is wise to be at least a half-hour late for a party—never be on time. If you know that the party will have a large attendance, feel free to arrive up to two hours late.

### Seating Etiquette

The host commonly sits at the head of the table. The guest of honor should sit at the other end of the table, opposite the host.

### Tipping Tips

Gratuities are not included in restaurant bills. Be sure to tip your server about 10 to 15 percent. Porters should be given $1 for each bag they carry. Taxi drivers commonly receive 10 percent of the fare.

### When You Are Invited to a Home

Panamanians love to entertain, so expect to be treated very warmly when visiting another person's home. Food is commonly served by a maid. It is inappropriate to volunteer to assist in clearing or washing dishes if the family has a maid. If they do not, you should provide such assistance.

It is common for Panamanians to entertain late into the night. Feel free to stay past midnight, even during the week.

### Women in Business

Women are enjoying more freedom in Panama and many are moving into managerial positions within local businesses. Foreign businesswomen should have little problem conducting business. However, men may still insist on paying for meals and this should be graciously allowed, unless you take measures to pay for the meal although away from the table.

### Whatever You Do....

- Don't be afraid to drink the water in Panama City. The water supply comes from the Canal Zone and is perfectly safe. However, outside the city, drink only bottled water.
- Don't be confused when you hear Panama City simply referred to as Panama.

- Don't neglect to make business appointments at least two weeks prior to your visit and to confirm meetings before your arrival.

- Don't make comments about how similar Panama is to the United States. Panamanians resent such comparisons.

- Don't fail to recognize that all inhabitants of North, Central, and South America are called "Americans." Do not refer to yourself or other U.S. citizens as Americans.

# Chapter 11

# Paraguay

## 8 reasons people do business in Paraguay

1. Paraguay is a producer and exporter of sugar cane.

2. An agricultural nation, Paraguay's major industries include the production and export of soybeans, cotton, timber, and meat.

3. The production of cement is also an important part of Paraguay's industry.

4. Paraguay has made great headway in overcoming its previous economic and political isolation from the rest of Latin America.

5. The country is a partner in the Mercosur Common Market, with hopes of opening up new agricultural and industrial opportunities.

6. The people of Paraguay emphasize peace over confrontation.

7. The government of this country is very supportive of the church.

8. Paraguay is home to some of the most beautiful wilderness in the world.

The Republic of Paraguay is one of the least-known countries of Latin America, due primarily to its centuries of isolation from the rest of the world. A major part of the reason for this is geographic; Paraguay has no coastline, but is "locked in" on all sides, by Argentina, Bolivia, and Brazil. In addition, much of its land is uninhabitable wilderness—fully 60 percent in a dry, arid region called the Chaco. Most of its population of 4.8 million people are compressed into the eastern portion of the country, where plateaus, grasslands, and forests also provide a beautiful and diverse environment for Paraguay's multiple (but fast-disappearing) species of wildlife and vegetation.

Paraguay's earliest known inhabitants were the Guaraní Indians. In the 1500s, the Spanish began colonizing the country, but unlike other Latin American countries, they were "absorbed" by the native population and took on Guaraní foods and customs. Nevertheless, Jesuit missionaries succeeded in "civilizing" the Indians, who learned many European arts and crafts along the road to conversion. This peaceful mingling of cultures has given Paraguay a unique identity among its South American neighbors.

Another contributing factor to that identity, however, was the rule of dictator José Gaspar Rodríguez de Francia—a.k.a. "El Supremo"—who took control of the country after Paraguay became independent of Spain in 1811. Shutting off the borders and allowing no interaction with other South American citizens, Francia essentially closed off Paraguay from the rest of the world. After his death in 1840, Antonio López began the necessary steps to modernize Paraguay and bring it back into contact with other nations.

However, his own successor, Antonio López Jr., offset all his work by entering into a war against Argentina, Brazil, and Uruguay (the Triple Alliance) that proved to be disastrous. Lasting from 1864 to 1870, this war resulted in the loss of major chunks of Paraguayan territory and many lives. Recovery from this episode has been slow and punctuated by disputes with other countries, particularly Bolivia, which laid claims to large parts of the Chaco.

The rise of the dictator Higinio Morínigo in 1940 led to a number of improvements in public health, transportation, and schooling, but his regime was oppressive to political opponents and frequently faced uprisings Morínigo was overthrown in 1948; a series of brief and unstable governments ensued.

From 1954 to 1989, self-appointed president General Alfredo Stroessner ruled, often brutally, until he too was overthrown and replaced by another general, Andrés Rodriguez. Rodriguez quickly instituted a series of reforms, bringing Paraguay back into the modern world and restoring peace and stability for a period of time.

Although the Colorado Party remains in power, assassinations and corruption have continued to mar the Paraguayan democracy and its way of life, even though it has come a long way from its isolationist days.

In 1995, it became a partner, with Argentina, Brazil, and Uruguay, in the Mercosur Common Market, although the results of this association have yet to be determined.

# Statistics and Information

### Air Travel

Paraguay's major airport is Silvio Pettirossi International Airport, located nine miles from Asunción's center. Taxis to the city cost around $15. Buses leave every 15 minutes and cost only 30 cents.

### Country Codes

Paraguay's country code is 595.

City codes:

- 21 for Asunción.
- 31 for Concepción.

### Currency

The currency of Paraguay is called the *guaraní*. Coins come in denominations of 50, 10, 5, and 1 *guaraníes* and bills come in denominations of 10,000, 5,000, 1,000, 500, and 100.

The best exchange rates can be found at banks or street changers. Note that automated teller machines may not recognize foreign credit cards.

### Dates

Just as in other Latin American countries, dates are written with the day preceding the month, then the year. Thus, January 30, 1999 would be written 30/1/99. If this date is being written out, it should appear as "el 30 de enero de 1999."

### Ethnic Makeup

Paraguay is the most homogenous country in South America. More than 95 percent of its inhabitants are mestizo, although the remainder of the population is made up of Italian,

German, and Japanese. Of these, the country has a particularly large German community.

## Holidays and Religious Celebrations

| | |
|---|---|
| January 1 | New Year's Day |
| February 3 | Feast of San Blas, Patron Saint of Paraguay |
| March 1 | Heroes' Day |
| Mid-April | Easter Weekend |
| May 1 | Labor Day |
| May 14/15 | Independence Day |
| 8th Thurs. in May | Corpus Christi/After Easter |
| June 12 | Chaco Armistice Day |
| August 15 | Founding of Asunción |
| August 25 | Constitution Day |
| September 29 | Victory of Boquerón Day |
| October 12 | Columbus Day |
| November 1 | All Saints Day |
| December 8 | Feast of the Virgin of Caacupé |
| December 25 | Christmas Day |

## Language

There are two official languages in Paraguay. Both Spanish and Guaraní, a native Indian dialect, are spoken widely. However, most members of the business community utilize Spanish as their primary language and many are familiar with English.

## Religion

Paraguay's state religion is Roman Catholicism. Although 97 percent of Paraguayans follow this religion, the government supports freedom of religion and does not suppress other faiths.

### Time Zone Differences

Paraguay is:

- Three hours behind Greenwich Mean Time.
- Two hours ahead of U.S. Eastern Standard Time.

### Weather

The eastern portion of Paraguay, where most of the population lives, experiences humidity and equal amounts of rainfall throughout the year. It is important to remember that because the country is located in the southern hemisphere, the seasons are the reverse of those in the U.S. The summer months (December through February) are hot and dry, although the winter is mild, with July being the coldest month of the year.

# Etiquette

### Business Attire

Paraguayans take great pride in their appearance. Even citizens of the lower classes are well groomed and dressed appropriately. Dress is conservative, with consideration given to the often hot, humid weather.

For business purposes, men should wear dark suits, white shirts, and ties. Women should wear professional-looking dresses and suits. Women may leave nylons at home during the hottest months.

### Business Entertaining/Dining

Dinner is the most common time for business entertaining. This meal is served much later in Paraguay than what you may be used to, often not beginning until 10 p.m. and lasting until after midnight. Because dinner is considered a purely social occasion, you should discuss business only if your counterpart initiates such a conversation.

At a restaurant, obtain your waiter's attention by saying *"mozo."* It is common for the person who asks the waiter for the bill to pay for the meal. Do offer politely to pay for your portion of the bill, but expect to be refused.

Dining is done continental style, with your fork held in your left hand and your knife in your right throughout the meal. In addition, your hands should always remain visible—do not place them in your lap or anywhere out of sight.

## Conversation

Paraguayans are very friendly, interesting people who enjoy lively conversation. You may notice that they will stand much closer to you during conversation than you are accustomed to. Do not back away, as it may be perceived as a sign of rudeness.

Any information you can learn about Paraguay before your visit will impress your associates. Good topics of discussion include local culture, sports, and family. In addition, Paraguay has a complex system of hydroelectric dams, of which they are very proud, so be sure to inquire about them.

As in most countries, stay away from discussing politics of any sort.

## Gestures and Public Manners

Paraguayans have a strong sense of manners and conduct themselves properly in public. You should do likewise. Always exhibit excellent posture and keep your voice low during conversation. Sit only on chairs, and never prop up your feet on other pieces of furniture. Never take anyone's picture without obtaining permission first.

There are some gestures that have specific meanings in Paraguay:

- Do not make the American "okay" symbol or cross your fingers. These gestures are considered to be obscene.

- Do not wink in Paraguay unless you have sexual intentions.

- Tapping your chin with your index finger indicates that you don't know something.

- Nodding your head backwards indicates that you've forgotten something.

Note that restrooms can only be found in hotels and restaurants. It would be wise to carry tissues with you, as you will find obtaining any difficult.

### Gift-Giving Etiquette

Note that due to contraband activity, many gifts commonly purchased in the United States can be obtained at a much lower cost in Paraguay. It may be wise to wait and buy gifts once you are in the country.

Gifts should be given to express your thanks for a dinner invitation or for a kind gesture that was extended to you. When you do give a gift, be sure to select a practical one. Some favorites include small electronic gadgets such as calculators, cameras, or tape recorders. If you are invited to a home, bring along some wine, chocolate, or flowers.

Do not give gifts of a knife or letter opener, as they are perceived as a sign of "cutting ties."

### Greetings and Introductions

Shaking hands is the proper form of greeting in Paraguay. Handshakes are considered very important and should be exchanged with everyone in attendance, both upon your arrival and at your departure.

Titles are important to Paraguayans. Always address another person by his or her appropriate title, unless you have been invited to use a less formal address. *Licenciado* is the title bestowed upon anyone who has received a college degree. Those with professional degrees, such as lawyers, doctors, professors, and architects, should be addressed as such.

## How Decisions are Made

Negotiations and decision making will move much slower in Paraguay than they do in the U.S.

Take the time to establish a strong personal relationship with your Paraguayan associates, and you will find that it will greatly influence your business negotiations.

## Meeting Manners

Attempt to schedule your meetings during the morning hours. This is the time of day that Paraguayans are at their best and will focus on giving you their undivided attention.

Expect meetings to begin late and to start with small talk. Never rush to get to the heart of the business matter, but wait until you have spent some time on personal relationships first.

Have all of your presentation literature and materials translated into Spanish. Business cards should be written in English on one side and in Spanish on the other.

## Punctuality

Although meetings rarely begin as scheduled, foreign businesspeople are expected to be on time.

## Seating Etiquette

There are no strict rules governing seating in Paraguay. However, it is common for the guest of honor to sit at the head of the table.

## Tipping Tips

Tipping is not as commonplace in Paraguay as it is in the U.S. However, because a gratuity is not included in a restaurant bill, it is appropriate to give your waiter a 10 percent tip.

Although it is not necessary, you may tip your cab driver 10 percent of the fare. Porters should be given 75 *guaraníes* as a tip.

## When You Are Invited to a Home

Remember never to stop by a Paraguayan's home during the afternoon hours. This is the time reserved for dining with the family, followed by a siesta.

In homes of the well-to-do, you will be served and catered to by the family's maid. Your hosts will be pleased if you eat plentifully and finish everything on your plate. You should plan on staying one to two hours after a meal for *maté* (Paraguay's favorite beverage) and conversation; never rush out at a meal's conclusion.

It is appropriate to thank your hosts for their hospitality by reciprocating with an invitation to dinner in a fine restaurant.

## Women in Business

Women constitute a strong 40 percent-plus of Paraguay's labor force. Many Paraguayan women hold professional degrees. Due to the strong sense of respect that Paraguayan men have for women, they find it difficult to argue or say no to a female colleague (or loved one). This can work to the advantage of a foreign businesswoman.

## Whatever You Do...

- Don't plan to eat at times common in the U.S. Paraguayans eat their main meal of the day at 2 p.m. and a light supper around 10 p.m.

- Don't forget that most businesses are closed during the afternoon hours of noon to 3 p.m.

- Don't eat fruits and vegetables that have not been peeled; harmful chemicals may be present on the skin.

- Don't drink the water or use ice cubes. Bottled or boiled water is the only safe water to consume in Paraguay.

- Don't call yourself "American." Bear in mind that any inhabitant of North or South America is an American, something of which Paraguayans are acutely aware.

- Don't schedule your business trip during the summer months (and remember they are opposite of those in the U.S.); this is the time many Paraguayans take vacations.

- Do not send different company representatives on each successive business trip. Because personal relationships are crucial in Paraguayan business, sending someone new will restart the process and delay a successful conclusion.

# Chapter 12

# Peru

---

**8 reasons people do business in Peru**

1. Peru's geographical location near the Andes makes it appealing to foreign investors.

2. The country is rich in copper and petroleum.

3. Peruvians are a hard-working, industrious people.

4. Peru's government welcomes foreign investors.

5. Peru is a major importer of U.S. telecommunications equipment.

6. There is a natural gas site in the country.

7. Major industries include the production and export of pulp, paper, and chemicals, as well as oil and minerals.

8. The government of Peru is sensitive to improving human rights.

---

The Republic of Peru is one of the most beautiful and culturally rich nations in South America. It is best known for its ancient Incan remains, and for the Peruvian Andes, where millions of Indians still live a very old way of life. Two large mountain ranges, the Cordillera Occidental and the Cordillera Oriental, rise high over the lush countryside. A good half of Peru is taken up by the Amazon Basin, where tourists go to view tropical rainforests and the thousands of species and animal and plant life that distinguish the country.

Peru is bordered by Ecuador to the northwest, Colombia on the north, Brazil to the northeast, Bolivia to the southeast, and Chile on the south. Its lengthy westernmost border lies along the Pacific Ocean. The oldest known human settlement in Peru dates back to 12,000 B.C. Around 1526, the Incans were already the dominant culture when the Spanish conquistadors, led by Francisco Pizarro, entered the country. The Incans also had become an extremely wealthy nation, as Pizarro quickly saw, and a few years later he returned with an army to subdue the Indians and exert Spanish control over the land. Incan resistance proved futile, and by 1534, Pizarro had succeeded in his mission. He founded Peru's capital city of Lima in 1535. In 1541, Pizarro was assassinated, but Spain continued to rule the country for the next 200 years, with Lima serving as a center of commerce and diplomatic relations among all the countries in that region of South America.

Although Peru was content under Spanish rule (with the exception of the Incans, who continued to exercise periodic rebellions against their oppressors), in 1824 Simón Bolivar and José de San Martin liberated the country. The now-independent nation subsequently entered into border and territory disputes with its neighbors, particularly Chile and Ecuador, that resulted in some losses and some gains. As the years passed into the 20th century, the once-placid country became increasingly beset by a series of political and economic upheavals, capped in 1965 by a number of unsuccessful guerrilla attacks led by the National Liberation Army and then followed in the 1980s by insurrections from other leftist guerilla groups.

In 1992, many guerilla leaders were captured, thus restoring hope for civil peace that was further buoyed by the 1990 election of Alberto Fujimoro as Peru's president. Fujimoro has been largely successful in his efforts to bring stability back into Peru's government and economy, although unemployment remains high and border disputes continue.

# Statistics and Information

### Air Travel

Lima's international airport is called the Jorge Chavez International Airport. It is less than seven miles from the heart of the city. Both buses and taxis will be available to get you from the airport to your destination.

### Country Codes

Peru's country code is 51.

City codes:

- 1 for Lima.
- 84 for Cuzco.

## Currency

Peru's currency is called the *nuevo sol*. Its coins are called *centavos*. One *nuevo sol* is equivalent to 100 centavos. Bills are available in denominations of 10,000, 5,000, 1,000, 500, 100, 50, 10, and 5 soles. Coins are available in 50 centavos, as well as in 100, 50, 10, 5, and 1 *soles*.

There are any number of options for changing money—banks, *cambios*, or hotels, with cambios probably offering the most convenience and best rates. Avoid the money changers on the street, as they have been known to cheat foreigners. Credit cards are generally accepted, but there is a high commission rate for using them.

## Dates

As in other Latin American countries, the European standard format style of writing dates is used in Peru: day, month, year. For instance, February 25, 2010 would be listed as 25.2.10. Written in longhand, this date would be "el 25 de *febrero* de 2010."

## Ethnic Makeup

Peru leads other Latin American countries when it comes to having the highest percentage of Quechua Indians (54 percent). In addition, approximately 32 percent of Peru's population are mestizo, although 12 percent is of Spanish descent, and the remainder is composed of blacks and Asians.

## Holidays and Religious Celebrations

| | |
|---|---|
| January 1 | New Year's Day |
| May 1 | Labor Day |
| July 28/29 | Independence Day |
| August 30 | Saint Rosa of the Americas |
| October 8 | Navy Day |
| November 1 | All Saints' Day |

December 8    Immaculate Conception

December 25  Christmas Day

## Language

Both Spanish and the Incan language called Quechua are heard frequently in Peru. Nearly one half of the population speak Quechua. Because many Peruvians who do business internationally have mastered English, you will hear that language spoken.

## Religion

The majority of Peruvians (90 percent) are Roman Catholic. Others follow various Protestant faiths or the beliefs of their Indian heritages.

## Time Zone Differences

Peru is:

- Five hours behind Greenwich Mean Time.
- The same as Eastern Standard Time.

## Weather

Although Peru is located in the tropics, its weather varies according to the geographic region. Generally, there is a wet and a dry season, as in many South American countries. Although the temperatures are quite comfortable throughout the year, the climate tends to be cooler near the mountains and hot and humid in areas around the tropical rainforests.

# Etiquette

## Business Attire

Business professional attire is the order of the day in Peru. Men should wear conservative suits during the work week, as well as during evening engagements. Women should prepare to wear suits or dresses in a tailored style accentuated with jewelry and make-up. Colored nail polish is also acceptable in the business arena.

### Business Card Etiquette

Be sure to get your business card printed in Spanish before going to Peru; it will please your Peruvian contacts to know that you've made this effort. If you have a title such as "Doctor," "Engineer," or "Professor," be sure include it under your name on your business card.

### Business Entertaining/Dining

You will find that the largest meal of the day is lunch, which is eaten around 12:30 p.m. This meal will consist of several courses, beginning with soup and ending with fruit for dessert.

If you have been invited to have tea or *la merienda*, you will be given the equivalent of a light snack. This meal is meant to satisfy your appetite until you have dinner much later in the evening.

When you are extending a dinner invitation, be sure to suggest that you meet around 9 p.m., which is the typical dinner hour in Peru. Because it is considered proper to be "fashionably late," prepare for your Peruvian guests to arrive closer to 9:30 p.m. After the meal has been completed, your guests will visit with you for 30 minutes or more before taking their leave.

Peruvians follow the continental style of dining, with the fork retained in the left hand and the knife in the right hand. When they have completed a course, the fork and knife are laid across the plate with the fork up and the serrated edge of the knife facing the person who has used it.

It is appropriate to eat all of the food that has been served to you, rather than leaving some of it on your plate (as is proper in other countries).

You will find that beer is the most common alcoholic beverage in Peru. If alcohol affects you, be conservative with the number of drinks that you have, because Peruvian beer tends to be rather strong. A very common nonalcoholic beverage that you will be offered is lemonade.

## Conversation

Appropriate topics of conversation include asking about your Peruvian contact's family and telling about your own family. Other good subjects to discuss are the sights you've seen in Peru and restaurants of interest in the particular area you are visiting.

Topics to avoid include Peruvian politics, drugs, and an individual's ethnic background, especially if they are of Indian descent. Raising any of these subjects may unknowingly cause offense. It is also considered rude to discuss a person's wages or prices that have been paid for items.

## Gestures and Public Manners

Just as in most other Latin American countries, your Peruvian contacts will take notice of where you will be staying. For that reason, be sure to stay in a hotel that is well respected according to Peruvian standards.

Although haggling is appropriate in some Latin American countries such as Mexico, this is not the case in Peru.

Note that when asking Peruvians how to get to a specific location, they will give you the way they *think* you should go, rather than knowing for sure. The best way to confirm correct directions is to ask a few different individuals.

## Gift-Giving Etiquette

Although gifts are not an essential part of establishing rapport during the first few meetings with your Peruvian contacts, you should definitely go with some things in hand. Because wine is a costly item in Peru, this would certainly be a well-received gift. In addition, time management tools (such as planners), books about your country, quality pen sets, and desk accessories make terrific presents.

Gifts to avoid include letter openers or any item with a sharp edge; these items are associated with severing ties. Also, do not give handkerchiefs, which are equated with mourning.

### Greetings and Introductions

When first meeting and greeting your Peruvian contacts, a confident handshake is in order. Once you have established rapport with your contacts, men may receive a hug although women may receive a kiss on each cheek. When you are greeted with more than a handshake, this is a sign that you have been accepted by these individuals.

### Hierarchy Is Important

Although you may meet many people within an organization, you will be able to determine the company's pecking order based on the titles (and possible ages) of the individuals you meet. When in doubt, take note of who defers to whom; this alone should enable you to identify the most senior person in a Peruvian organization.

### How Decisions are Made

Even though many people may be involved in your meetings, the most senior manager in attendance will have the final say. For that reason, it will be important to defer to that person and cultivate your relationship with him. This is particularly true because in most cases, aside from who has the best service or product, the determining factor in a Peruvian's decision will be which person has been the best at establishing and maintaining rapport.

### Meeting Manners

When scheduling meetings, be sure to arrange only one during the day. If possible, request your meeting time to be during the middle of the morning.

Note that although many of your Peruvian colleagues may have a working knowledge of English, they will appreciate it when your presentation material has been prepared in their native language.

## Punctuality

Just as in many other Latin American countries, the concept of *la hora latina* exists in Peru. Thus, you will find your Peruvian contacts to be more relaxed about time than individuals in many other parts of the world. Although you will be expected to arrive punctually for business meetings, you may be kept waiting for 15 to 30 minutes or longer.

When you are invited to a social gathering, it is considered good manners to arrive approximately 30 minutes after the time you were invited.

## Seating Etiquette

In any formal function, you will find that the host will be seated at the head of the table. If a hostess is present, she will sit opposite the host. The most senior female guest will be seated to the immediate right of the host, although the most senior male will be seated to the immediate left of the hostess.

## Tipping Tips

Most restaurants in Peru will include a 15 percent service charge with the bill. If the service was outstanding, be sure to tip an additional amount.

When you are using a taxi for transportation, it is not necessary to tip over and above the fare.

Porters should receive the equivalent of $1 when they assist you with your luggage.

If you rent a car and stop at a gas station to refuel the gas tank, be sure to tip the attendant a few centavos.

## Toasting Etiquette

When you are engaged in business luncheons or dinners, you will probably be offered an alcoholic beverage. If a toast is made during this occasion, be sure to reciprocate by proposing one in return. The best form to follow is to lift your goblet and say, "Salud!"

## When You Are Invited to a Home

Consider it an honor if you are invited to your Peruvian contact's home. Be sure to arrive later than the time of the invitation; if you arrive early, or even on time, it may embarrass your host, who may not be prepared to receive you.

You should also go with a gift in hand. Your host's spouse will probably enjoy quality chocolates from your homeland. If your host has children, take along a gift from your favorite sports team or toys that children in your own country would enjoy receiving.

## Women in Business

Although Peruvian women have made great strides in the world of business, Peruvian men still conduct the majority of their business dealings with other men. For that reason, women from abroad who are doing business in Peru should put their most professional selves forward both in their demeanor and their dress and be patient with attitudes of machismo they may encounter. By doing so, they will be taken more seriously.

## Whatever You Do...

- Don't forget to be tactful and diplomatic in Peru. If you are too direct, Peruvians will not value what you have to say.

- Don't wear tennis shoes or shorts except if you are going to work out at a gym or visiting the beach. Casual clothes, especially business casual, are not considered proper attire in Peru.

- Don't bring up business during dinner engagements. Confine yourself to social topics instead.

- Don't forget that your title will assist you in gaining clout with your Peruvian contacts. Therefore, be sure it is mentioned on your business cards and presentation materials.

- Don't give any items in an amount totalling 13. Just as in the United States, this number is considered bad luck.

- Don't forget that you probably will be in a higher altitude than normal when you are in Peru. Give yourself a chance to get accustomed to it.

- Don't motion for another to come near you by opening your hand and moving your fingers toward you. Instead, move your fingers back and forth with your hand facing the ground.

# Chapter 13

# Uruguay

---

**9 reasons people do business in Uruguay**

1. Uruguay lies in close proximity to Brazil and is also easily accessible to Argentina.

2. The country has no income tax.

3. Uruguay has a strong telecommunications industry.

4. Uruguay has a stable democratic government with a history of cooperation with the U.S.

5. The country is popular with tourists.

6. Uruguay is one of the world's largest producers of beef.

7. Uruguay has a strong agricultural economy; nearly 90 percent of the land is arable.

8. Granite and marble are two of Uruguay's most abundant resources. It is also rich in semiprecious stones.

9. Major exports include fish, meat, wool, rice, sugar, and manufactured goods.

---

The Oriental Republic of Uruguay, South America's second smallest country, lies on the southeastern coast of the continent, essentially "tucked in" to its position by Brazil on the north and Argentina on the west. To the south is the mouth of the Rio de la Plata, on which lies the capital city of Montevideo. The countryside consists mostly of grasslands punctuated by two small mountain ranges, the Cuchilla de Haedo and the Cuchilla Grande. Along the coastline, Uruguay boasts some beautiful beaches and dunes, but otherwise the landscape is unimpressive and the wildlife is rare.

Uruguay is one of the few South American countries that was not conquered by the Spanish in the 1500s. Rather, the native Charrua Indians killed initial explorers. However, by the mid-1600s, the Charrua had begun to enter into trade agreements with Spain, and Portugal soon followed. Both European countries soon established colonies, and in due time Uruguayan resistance against the intruders culminated in the emergence of José Artigas as the country's liberator and leader.

In 1828, Uruguay was established as an independent state and began an uncertain period during which internal factions (called the Blancos and the Colorados) warred with each other for economic and political control of the country.

Finally, in the early 1900s, a new President, José Battle y Ordóñez succeeded in overcoming opposition and establishing a series of reforms. With help from its strong agricultural sector, the country gradually achieved peace and economic success. However, this stability became threatened during the 1960s by increasing corruption and the rise of new guerrilla movements. In 1971, the military interceded and took the reigns of government away from Congress, which was dissolved. Democracy did not return to Uruguay until the presidential elections of 1984. Because then, the country has made significant headway in its return to economic and political stability.

Although not a giant on the political scene in South America, Uruguay has exerted its share of cultural influence via the international renown achieved by its writers, artists, and musicians. Additionally, the country is distinguished by having the highest literacy rate (94 percent) on the continent.

# Statistics and Information

### *Air Travel*

The MVD/Montevideo International Airport is Uruguay's main airport, located approximately 20 miles from Montevideo. If you choose to take a bus from the airport to the city, it will run approximately $6; if you choose to take a taxi, it will run approximately $30.

### *Country Codes*

Uruguay's country code is 598.

City codes:

- 2 for Montevideo.
- 342 for San Jose.

## Currency

The unit of currency in Uruguay is called the *peso*. Notes are found in amounts of 10,000, 5,000, 1,000, 500, 100, and 50. Coins circulate in denominations of 10, 5, 2, and 1 *peso*.

When on the Uruguayan coast, the best place to change money is in the *cambios* found in the cities and beach resorts. If you are in the interior, you will need to go to a bank. You cannot use your credit cards in Uruguayan automated teller machines.

## Dates

Uruguayans write their dates in the European standard format style of day, month, and year. For example, January 30, 1999 would be written as 30/1/99.

## Ethnic Makeup

Approximately 88 percent of Uruguay's population is of European descent, although 8 percent are mestizo and 4 percent are black.

## Holidays and Religious Celebrations

| | |
|---|---|
| January 1 | New Year's Day |
| January 6 | Epiphany |
| February/March | Carnival |
| March/April | Holy Thursday and Easter Sunday |
| April 19 | The Landing of 33 Uruguayans |
| May 1 | Labor Day |
| May 18 | Memorial of the Las Piedras Battle |
| June 19 | Anniversary of the Birth of Artigas |
| July 18 | Constitution Day |
| August 25 | Independence Day |
| October 12 | Columbus Day |
| November 1 | All Souls' Day |

| December 8 | Immaculate Conception |
| December 25 | Christmas |

Besides being an ideal time for vacationing, the months of December through April also mark a number of important holidays. If possible, avoid conducting business during these months. Also, be sure to check the region you are visiting for local holidays and practices.

As in many other Latin American countries, the Carnival celebration is accompanied by the throwing of water balloons. Be aware that if you happen to be within throwing distance, you may be a likely target.

## Language

Spanish is Uruguay's official language. However, the Spanish dialect spoken by Uruguayans contains a strong Italian influence. Consequently, those who speak classical Spanish may experience some difficulty when conversing.

*Note*: In some cities that border Brazil, a Uruguayan dialect known as *fronterizo* is spoken. This dialect is a combination of Spanish and Portuguese.

## Religion

About 66 percent of the population is Roman Catholic, 2 percent is Protestant, and 2 percent is Jewish. The remaining 28 percent of the population do not practice a specific religious belief.

## Times Zone Differences

Uruguay is:

- Three hours behind Greenwich Mean Time.

- Two hours ahead of Eastern Standard Time.

### Weather

Uruguay has relatively the same temperate climate throughout each of its regions. Expect warm temperatures accompanied by humidity during the summer and a cold, wet climate during the winter months.

# Etiquette

### Business Attire

Uruguayans dress in accordance with the temperature. Be sure to wear light materials in the summer that are compatible with the humidity you are likely to encounter. In winter months, it is advisable to bring a rain jacket.

For business dress, men should wear dark-colored suits and conservative ties. Women should wear skirts, conservative business suits, and dresses, as well as quality shoes. Both men and women should avoid bright or flashy colors. Stick with dark, conservative attire.

Be sure to dress conservatively when entertaining or being entertained, especially because many restaurants have a formal dress code. Suits or jackets with a tie would be the norm. Skirts and blouses or elegant dresses are acceptable for women.

### Business Card Etiquette

Be sure to bring along plenty of business cards, which should be printed in Spanish on the opposite side. Exchange cards with everyone you meet in a business setting. Present your card, Spanish side up, so that your cross cultural associate can read the card as it is being received.

### Business Entertaining/Dining

Breakfast typically is eaten sometime between 7 a.m. and 8 a.m., lunch between noon and 2:30 p.m., and dinner between 8:30

p.m. and 10:30 p.m. Both business lunches and dinners are usually common.

Always allow your host to take the lead in conversations. If you happen to be the host, keep in mind that Uruguayans often perceive business meals as social occasions. As a result, you should patiently "test the waters" to see if any business discussion would be appropriate.

Always arrive on time when meeting for a business meal. Be on your best behavior when dining in Uruguay. Like most Latin Americans, Uruguayans value proper etiquette.

Don't refuse any food you are offered. Instead, be polite and try to taste everything you encounter. However, note that medical and religious reasons are always an acceptable excuse not to eat certain foods.

Always offer food to others before serving yourself. Don't chew with your mouth open or speak with a mouthful of food.

If you want to get the attention of your waiter, discreetly extend your hand into the air and make eye contact.

If you happen to be the host, be aware that restaurants serving Uruguayan, Italian, and French cuisines often are favored. It would be wise to ask your hotel concierge for the names of prestigious restaurants in your area.

### Conversation

Uruguayans are vibrant conversationalists. Prepare for interesting talk and enthusiastic attitudes about a variety of subjects. Don't be surprised if you are interrupted frequently.

Good topics of conversation include: Uruguay's sightseeing locations; the positive aspects of Uruguay's history; your counterpart's choice of music; culture; international politics; vacations; sports such as volleyball, soccer, and basketball; and food and wine.

Avoid asking personal or probing questions. Do not ask questions concerning family life, a person's professional status, salary, or religion. Above all, never say anything negative concerning Uruguay, as the majority of its people are very patriotic. In particular, avoid any criticism of Uruguayan sports, especially soccer.

### Gestures and Public Manners

One common gesture in Uruguay is to make a fist and extend the thumb. This means "OK." Another is to scrape your fingers underneath your chin, which communicates "I don't know" or "I don't care."

Always maintain good eye contact when meeting and greeting or when conversing with others. Cover your mouth when sneezing, coughing, yawning, etc.

Never insult or attempt to mock Uruguayans, especially in public. The people of Uruguay are very proud and will be greatly offended, putting an abrupt end to your business endeavor.

### Gift-Giving Etiquette

Giving a gift on a first encounter is typically a nice gesture. Be aware, however, that gift-giving is not a popular practice in Uruguay. It may be advisable to develop close friendships before exchanging gifts.

Good gifts to give include quality pen sets, gifts native to your homeland, fine wines and other well-known brands of alcohol, office accessories, or artistic items for the home. Make your gift unique rather than something easily attainable in Uruguay.

Avoid giving items that may seem to be too personal or practical to your Uruguayan counterparts, or anything expensive or extravagant. Although you should always give quality items, use your good judgment to avoid embarrassing any of your crosscultural colleagues.

## Greetings and Introductions

Be sure to shake hands with everyone you encounter. Handshakes should be sincere and inviting. If possible, avoid group greetings. It is more appropriate to greet people as individuals.

Greetings in Uruguay often entail some level of affection. Backpatting and arm touching are common. Initial business greetings may be somewhat formal and require less physical contact, yet will still maintain warmth and enthusiasm.

Be prepared for casual conversation and pleasantries when meeting somebody for the first time. Allow your Uruguayan counterpart to set the tone.

Uruguayans often stand at a closer proximity when greeting and conversing. Try to avoid backing away; it may be perceived as insulting.

## Hierarchy Is Important

As is often the case, there is a definite "pecking order" in Uruguayan companies. You should be able to determine most of the high-ranking people both by the presence they command and the respect shown to them by their employees. Another clue for finding out "who is who" is by looking at the titles on the business cards you receive.

## How Decisions are Made

As in most Latin American countries, decisions are made at the top. These decisions will be based on group consensus and the relationships you have forged. Uruguayans are just as interested in the person doing the negotiating as the product or benefits your company offers.

Play it safe; show people at all levels of the company proper respect and personal interest. Your ability to conduct successful business will be determined by your ability to build personal friendships.

Uruguayans are often sensitive to the cultural differences between Latin Americans and North Americans. As a result, negotiations may tend to move faster when they deal with foreigners and decisions may be reached faster than in other Latin American countries.

## Meeting Manners

Typically, meetings in Uruguay involve a significant amount of small talk and socializing. Always let your counterparts set the pace and initiate any business conversation. Expect business meetings to be conducted in a formal setting.

Be sure to have all material translated into Spanish before your arrival. It is also advisable to hire an interpreter, even if your Uruguayan counterparts can speak English at some level.

Uruguayans tend to deal with business upfront, and do not attempt to "sugar coat" their fears, decisions, and rejections. This is especially true when they are dealing with North Americans and is something to keep in mind as you conduct negotiations.

Be sure to give the appropriate recognition to the key decision maker as you engage in meetings.

## Punctuality

As an individual from abroad, you should always be on time when meeting with your crosscultural colleagues. Don't expect your Uruguayan counterparts to be punctual, however. It is possible they will attempt to be on time out of respect for North American customs, but it shouldn't be expected. Allow Uruguayan associates to be 20 to 30 minutes late.

## Seating Etiquette

Seating etiquette in Uruguay dictates that the host will seat himself at the head of the table and offer the seat to his immediate right to his most senior guest. The person co-hosting the meeting will typically take the seat across from the host and invite the second most senior guest to be seated to his immediate right.

## Tipping Tips

Restaurants may or may not include a gratuity depending on the specific location and size of your party. If no gratuity has been added to your bill, then it is appropriate to add on a tip of 10 to 15 percent.

Porters should be given $1 U.S. for each piece of luggage that is handled.

Taxi drivers should be given a 10 percent tip. Ask your hotel concierge to estimate the fare for the distance you are traveling. You may also consider asking the driver to estimate the fare to your destination before leaving.

## Toasting Etiquette

Etiquette dictates that glasses be raised when others are proposing a toast; the only person who should allow the glass to remain on the table is the person being toasted. Once the toast has been made, the recipient should propose a toast in return to his table companions.

## When You Are Invited to a Home

If invited to a Uruguayan home, it is polite to send flowers, candy, or perhaps a fruit basket before the occasion. Roses, often a favorite gift, do not contain the same romantic connotations as they do in the United States.

You should arrive 30 to 45 minutes late, unless otherwise specified. Dress in conservative, formal attire when invited to a home (for men a dark suit or jacket and tie). Remember, it is always better to err on the side of formality.

Don't over-stay your welcome when visiting someone's home. Be sensitive to your host's needs and depart at the appropriate time. However, avoid leaving abruptly; this may be interpreted as an insult. Instead, slowly make the transition to depart. Be aware that when coffee is served, this is often a hint that your visit is nearing an end.

## Women in Business

Uruguay is one of the few Latin American countries where women have made great strides. In fact, the opportunities open to them equal what their male counterparts have.

Uruguayan women have many terrific role models in their country, including females in the government sector. For this reason, women traveling to Uruguay from abroad will find that they are accepted and respected.

## Whatever You Do...

- Don't underestimate the power of a local agent. Hiring an agent can often help incorporate you into the business arena and assist you in becoming aquainted with those who have decision-making power.

- Don't ever joke or use sarcasm around your crosscultural colleagues. Although humor is appreciated, it is often misunderstood.

- Don't ever assume that you can mistreat an individual simply because he or she is a lower-level employee. Show proper respect to all your Uruguayan associates.

- Don't underestimate the importance of staying in a prestigious hotel. As in many Latin American countries, Uruguayans may judge you by the hotel you choose.

- Don't attempt to do business before taking the time to develop a relationship. Be sure to communicate that people are your priority.

- Don't schedule back-to-back meetings. It is very common for meetings to begin late and end even later!

- Don't be surprised if introductions are somewhat physical (shoulder touching, arm patting and conversing in close proximity).

# Chapter 14

# Venezuela

---

**8 reasons people do business in Venezuela**

1. Venezuela is one of the biggest players in the oil export industry.

2. The country has a close diplomatic and economic relationship with the United States.

3. There are numerous world-renowned hotels in Venezuela.

4. The Venezuelan government encourages investments from abroad.

5. The country is rich in paper products.

6. Venezuela is a multicultural nation.

7. Fishing and agriculture are top industries.

8. Among its major industries are the production and export of petroleum and iron ore.

---

The Republic of Venezuela is located on the northernmost coast of South America, along the Caribbean Sea. It is bordered by Colombia on the west, Brazil on the south, and Guyana on the east. The country's diverse scenery includes miles of white sand beaches along the coast, the Guyana Highlands in the southeast, the Cordillera de los Andes in the western sections, and grasslands (called the Llanos) in the central plains; the lowlands in the northeast surround Lake Maracaibo, South America's largest inland lake. This country is also home to the third-longest river on the continent, the Orinoco, as well as Angel Falls, the highest waterfall on the planet, and innumerable species of plant life and wildlife. Caracas, the country's capital, lies near the north coast; close to 3.5 million people live there, although Venezuela itself has a population of more than 21 million.

Venezuela (translation: "Little Venice") was named by explorer Alonso de Ojeda, although Christopher Columbus was the first European to visit the country. As with other South American countries, Venezuela was originally populated by indigenous Indian tribes—the Caribam, the Arawak, and the Chibcha—whose numbers were decimated from disease and military conquest when the Spanish and Germans began colonizing the land. Spain eventually took control of the country, but was forced out by South America's great liberator, Simón Bolívar, in 1821. Bolívar had hoped to unify the countries of Venezuela, Ecuador, and Colombia into one nation called Gran Colombia, but after his death in 1830,

Venezuela declared its independence and his vision was never realized. Instead, the country would go on to be ruled by a series of dictators.

It was not until the early 1900s, when huge oil reserves were discovered in the Maracaibo basin, that the country began to experience a measure of economic prosperity, although poorer Venezuelans would continue to struggle with disease and illiteracy. In 1947, uprisings related to economic inequalities led to the establishment of a democratic government and free elections. Still, political conflicts and intrigues in the intervening years have been frequent and bitter, often centering on oil. A major event in both energy and politics occurred when Venezuela nationalized previously foreign-owned oil and iron companies in 1976. Serious economic problems (and political dissatisfaction) followed the decline in the world's oil prices of the early 1980s.

Many of Venezuela's economic and social challenges have stubbornly persisted. There have been frequent charges of governmental mismanagement and corruption, and there was a failed attempt at a military coup in 1992. In December of 1998, a new president, Hugo Chavez, was elected, and hopes now are for an economic recovery that will put Venezuela back at the forefront of the world's oil producers.

Leaving aside contentious social and political issues, one relates Venezuela's enduring appeal to outsiders. It has always been a popular attraction for tourists who enjoy its many scenic wonders and beautiful beaches.

# Statistics and Information

### *Air Travel*

When traveling to Venezuela, you may fly into the country's main airport, which is in Maiquetia. From here, it will take less than an hour to drive to the heart of Caracas. Although buses may be available, a more practical way is to have a taxi take you into the city.

## Country Codes

Venezuela's country code is 58.

City codes:

- 2 for Caracas, followed by a seven-digit number.
- 85 for Ciudad Bolivar, followed by a five- or six-digit number.
- 76 for San Cristobal, followed by a five- or six-digit number.
- 42 for Puerto Cabello, followed by a four-, five- or six-digit number.

## Currency

The *bolívar* (abbreviated *Bs*) is the official currency of Venezuela. One *bolívar* is equivalent to 100 *centimos*; one *real* is equivalent to 50 *centimos*; one *medio* is equivalent to 25 *centimos*. The *bolívar* comes in denominations of 5, 2, and 1.

Money can be changed at banks or at *casas de cambio*; the latter will deal only with cash, not travelers checks. Visa and MasterCard are also widely accepted.

## Ethnic Makeup

More than two-thirds (67 percent) of Venezuela 's population are mestizo, although 21 percent is of European descent, 10 percent of African descent, and 2 percent are Indians.

## Holidays and Religious Celebrations

| | |
|---|---|
| January 1 | New Year's Day |
| May 1 | Labor Day |
| June 24 | Battle of Carabobo |

July 5        Independence Day

July 24       Bolívar's Birthday

October 12    Columbus Day

December 8    Immaculate Conception

December 25   Christmas Day

## Language

The official language of Venezuela is Spanish. However, English is the language of business in Caracas and is also taught within the education system. Because Venezuela shares its southern border with Brazil, Portuguese is also commonly heard in the country's capital. There are also more than 30 Amerindian languages spoken throughout the country.

## Religion

The vast majority (96 percent) of Venezuelans are Roman Catholics, although most of the remainder practice Protestantism.

## Time Zone Differences

Venezuela is:

- Four hours behind Greenwich Mean Time.
- One hour ahead of U.S. Eastern Standard Time.

## Weather

Because Venezuela is located in the tropics, its temperatures vary based on altitude.

# Etiquette

## Business Attire

Just as in other Latin American countries such as Argentina and Mexico, Venezuelans are very fashion conscious; in fact, they follow European fashions closely. For that reason, be sure to dress in a conservative yet stylish manner. Pay close attention to accessories; these will be noticed and even impress your contacts if they are made by top designers.

## Business Card Etiquette

Business cards are an important part of developing a relationship with your Venezuelan contacts. For that reason, it is a good idea to have your cards translated into Spanish and to have them ready when first meeting others. Because Venezuelans are impressed by status, be sure to emphasize your title on your business card.

## Business Entertaining/Dining

An important part of developing a business relationship with your Venezuelan contact entails going out to eat together. This creates time to get to know each other on a personal level and should be regarded as a social occasion. Thus, you should avoid talking about business unless your Venezuelan contact initiates it.

Unlike other Latin American countries, lunchtime in Venezuela is usually between noon and 2 p.m. This meal will consist of five or more courses, including soup and dessert, followed by strong coffee.

When you receive a dinner invitation, prepare to eat around 9 p.m. and to enjoy a much lighter cuisine, similar to what people in the United States are likely to have at lunch.

No matter what meal you are sharing with your Venezuelan contact, the continental style of dining will be followed, with the fork in your left hand and the knife in your right at all times.

## Conversation

When talking to Venezuelans, be sure to let them know what you have liked most about their country. Most Venezuelans enjoy discussing their country's history, arts, and sports, especially baseball and soccer. Just as in many other countries, restaurants and food also make good topics for small talk.

Topics to avoid include asking about the other person's private life, religion, and Venezuelan politics.

## Gestures and Public Manners

Good posture is a must and should be maintained at all times, even when you are in relaxed situations.

Be forewarned that Venezuelans tend to stand very close to others, often less than two arms' lengths. Although this may feel like an invasion of privacy to you, remember that it is their comfort level and should be respected.

Just as in the United States, eye contact is an important way to tell others you are being attentive to them. It is therefore appropriate to maintain eye contact with your Venezuelan contacts both when they are talking and when you are sharing information with them.

Be sure to avoid pointing with your index finger; instead, use your entire hand.

## Gift-Giving Etiquette

Although gifts may not be part of the relationship-development process when first meeting your Venezuelan contact, they should be given after you have been invited to dinner or when someone has done something nice for you. Gifts that will be appreciated include a name brand pen or desk set. If you choose to send flowers, orchids are best and will be readily available, because that is the country's official flower.

Other appropriate gifts include fine chocolates and books that are on the *New York Times* bestseller list (if your contacts read English, of course), as well as anything involving electronics.

## Greetings and Introductions

An appropriate Venezuelan greeting consists of addressing others as *Señor, Señora* or *Señorita*, followed by their last names. As in most Latin American countries, Venezuelans will most likely have two last names, with the first being their father's name and the second their mother's last name; for example, José Ruiz García. Until your Venezuelan contact tells you how he/she would like to be addressed, be sure to use both names.

It goes without saying that individuals should not be addressed by their first name unless they have given you permission to do so.

The appropriate way to meet and greet others is by offering a confident handshake. Once you have established rapport with your Venezuelan contact, you may even receive an *abrazo*, or embrace.

## Hierarchy Is Important

In some privately owned Venezuelan organizations, hierarchy may be very well defined with a vertical pecking order. In other organizations, there may be a less defined hierarchical order. Use your best judgment to determine who has the most authority or decision-making power.

## How Decisions are Made

Many Venezuelan companies may be family-owned, especially the ones that have been in existence for several decades. In this case, probably the most senior family members will have the ultimate say about how decisions are made. In organizations that are not privately owned, decisions may be made by senior management along with the person who has the best expertise necessary for understanding the project being discussed.

## Meeting Manners

Be sure to confirm your meeting a few days before the actual date—fax or e-mail provides the most practical way to do this.

You will notice that small talk is an important part of the way that Venezuelans launch meetings. It also provides a means for becoming acquainted on a personal level. Even if you are ready to get down to business, allow your Venezuelan contacts to take the lead and do your best to cultivate the rapport you want to establish.

## Punctuality

Promptness will be expected of you in both business situations and social gatherings. It will be both noticed and appreciated if you show up on time, if not a little earlier.

## Seating Etiquette

In a social situation, you will notice that the host and hostess will be seated at opposite ends of the table. The most senior woman/guest of honor will be offered the seat to the right of the hostess although the most senior man will be asked to sit to the immediate right of the host.

## Tipping Tips

It is unnecessary to tip taxi drivers unless they have helped you with your luggage, in which case you should acknowledge them with the equivalent of a few dollars. Porters and skycaps should also be tipped the equivalent of $1 per bag handled.

Restaurants typically include a 10 percent service charge in the bill. If service was above and beyond your expectations, be sure to leave an additional 5 percent or so.

## Toasting Etiquette

Just as in other Latin American countries, the proper way to offer a toast is by lifting your goblet and saying "Salud!" or "To Your Health."

## When You Are Invited to a Home

Because most Venezuelans rarely entertain in their homes, you should consider it a great honor if you receive such an invitation. Therefore, be sure to go with a gift in hand for your contact and his/her family.

## Women in Business

You will find that Venezuelan women are in high-ranking positions in both government and business sectors. For that reason, Venezuelan men will be accustomed to doing business with women. Despite this, it is important to bear in mind that *machismo* is an important part of the Venezuelan male. Foreign businesswomen should be flattered by chivalric gestures they receive, yet they should maintain a professional demeanor at all times.

Although being professionally dressed is important, it is equally important to be very chic in appearance. This includes fine jewelry, heels, and make-up. Dressing with class will be noticed and may even be acknowledged.

## Whatever You Do...

- Don't wear shorts or tennis shoes in public unless you are on your way to the beach.
- Don't forget to write a thank-you note following a social get-together. Venezuelans choose to develop relationships with people with whom they have developed rapport and a letter of thanks is a way to build it.
- Don't be surprised if Venezuelans address you by a pet name that, when translated into English, may be a term you would never think of calling others (for example, *gordita*, which means fatty).
- Don't snack although you are walking. Instead, wait until you sit down before you eat.

- Don't be surprised if several people in the same company are related. This is very common in companies that have been established for a long time.
- Don't be the first to start making small talk. Instead, allow your Venezuelan counterpart to set the tone of the conversation.

# Conclusion

You now have read that it takes more to conduct business successfully outside your own country than merely greeting contacts and exchanging business cards. You probably have learned that there is a unique art to doing business in Latin America. I hope that you will make this book one of your travel companions when visiting this part of the world.

Do you have a question about Latin American business etiquette that was not addressed in this book? You can e-mail me at ateaselatinamerica@etiq.com or contact me by writing to At Ease Inc., 119 East Court Street, Cincinnati, Ohio 45202, or by calling 800-873-9909, or FAXing 978-777-6995. I can assure you of a prompt response.

## AT·EASE·INC·
### INTERNATIONAL DIVISION

## Latin America Etiquette HOTLINE

**WHAT ETIQUETTE QUESTIONS DO YOU HAVE ON....**
Appropriate Dress • Forms of Address • Punctuality
Topics To Avoid • Do's And Taboos • Women In Business
• Seating Etiquette • Gift-Giving Manners • Business Entertaining
• Public Manners • Tipping Tips • Women In Business

**E-Mail Your Questions To: latinamerica@ateaseinc.com
or Call Our U.S. Domestic Hotline At (800) 873-9909
Or Fax Your Questions To (513) 241-8701
Visit Our Website At: www.latinamericanetiquette.com
119 East Court Street • Cincinnati, Ohio 45202**

# Bibliography

Bosrock, Mary Murray. *Put Your Best Foot Forward in South America. A Fearless Guide to International Communication and Behavior*. Minnesota: International Education Systems, 1997.

Cramer, Mark. *Culture Shock! A Guide to Customs and Etiquette Bolivia*. Oregon Graphic Arts Center Publishing Company, 1996.

Cramer, Mark. *Culture Shock! A Guide to Customs and Etiquette. Chile*. Oregon: Graphic Arts Center Publishing Company, 1998.

Devine, Elizabeth, and Nancy L. Braganti. *The Traveler's Guide to Latin American Customs & Manners*. New York: St. Martin's Press, 1988.

Dresser, Norine. *Multicultural Manners: New Rules of Etiquette for a Changing Society*. New York: John Wiley & Sons, Inc., 1996.

Harrison, Phyllis A. *Behaving Brazilian. A Comparison of Brazilian and North American Social Behavior.* Massachusetts: Newbury House Publishers, 1983.

Hutchison, William R. and Cynthia A. Poznanski with Laura Todt-Stockman. *Living in Colombia. A Guide for Foreigners.* Maine: Intercultural Press Inc., 1987.

Malat, Randy. *Passport Mexico. Your Pocket Guide to Mexican Business, Customs and Etiquette.* California: World Trade Press, 1996.

Morrison, Terri with Wayne A. Conaway and Joseph J. Douress. *Dun & Bradstreet's Guide to Doing Business Around the World.* New Jersey: Prentice Hall, 1997.

Allen, Derek. *Addressing Overseas Business Letters.* Great Britain: St. Edmundsbury Press, 1988.

Axtell, Roger, with Tami Briggs, Margaret Corcoran and Mary Beth Lamb. *Do's and Taboos Around the World for Women in Business.* New York: John Wiley & Sons, Inc., 1997.

Axtell, Roger. *Do's and Taboos Around the World. Compiled by The Parker Pen Company.3rd edition.* New York: John Wiley & Sons, Inc. 1993.

Axtell, Roger. *Do's and Taboos of Hosting International Visitors.* New York: John Wiley & Sons, Inc., 1990.

Jessup, Jay and Maggie Jessup. *Doing Business in Mexico.* California: Prima Publishing, 1993.

Morrison, Terri with Wayne A. Conway and George A. Borden, Ph.D. *Kiss, Bow, or Shake Hands.* Massachusetts: Adams Media Corporation, 1994.

# About the Author

Ann Marie Sabath is the president of At Ease Inc., a 14-year-old Cincinnati-based company specializing in domestic and international business etiquette programs.

She is also the author of *Business Etiquette In Brief; Business Etiquette: 101 Ways To Conduct Business With Charm And Savvy; International Business Etiquette: Asia & The Pacific Rim* and *International Business Etiquette: Europe.*

Sabath's international and domestic business etiquette concepts have been featured in the *Wall Street Journal, USA Today* and Delta Airlines' *Sky* Magazine. They also have been recognized on The Oprah Winfrey Show , 20/20, CNN and CNBC.

Since 1987, Sabath and her staff have trained more than 30,000 individuals representing the business, industry, government and educational sectors in how to gain the competitive edge.

Her *10 Key Ways For Enhancing Your Global Savvy, Polish That Builds Profits, Business Etiquette: The Key To Effective Services* and Programs have been presented to individuals representing Deloitte & Touche LLP, Fidelity Investments, General Electric, Procter & Gamble, Arthur Andersen, MCI Telecommunications, The Marriott Corporation, Salomon Brothers, and Technicolor among others.

In 1992, At Ease Inc. became an international firm by licensing its concept in Taiwan. In 1998, this firm also established its presence in Egypt, Australia and Slovakia by certifying individuals in these countries. Her forthcoming book, *Beyond Business Casual-What To Wear To Work If You Want To Get Ahead,* will be released in Spring 2000.

# Index